Hyperfocus
An Anthology
Spectrum Writing

Argonautica Press

First published in 2024 by Argonautica Press

PO Box 481, Ashburton, VIC 3147, Australia

www.argonauticapress.com

Spectrum Writing acknowledges that the lands these stories are told upon are the traditional lands of the Kaurna people and that we respect their spiritual relationship with their country.

We also acknowledge the Kaurna people as the custodians of the Adelaide region and that their cultural and heritage beliefs are still as important to the living Kaurna people today.

We also pay respects to the cultural authority of Aboriginal people visiting/attending from other areas of South Australia/Australia.

Edited by ©E.K. Earle 2024

Cover and illustrations by ©Adara Frances 2024

Hyperfocus stories ©individual authors 2024

ISBN:

978-0-6484787-8-2 (paperback)

978-0-6484787-9-9 (ebook)

Supported by a grant from the Office for Autism, Government of South Australia.

Government of South Australia

Office for Autism

contents

Foreword

It's a beautiful moment for me to write this foreword, and in some ways, it's a love letter to myself and others from that forgotten generation of autistic creatives in Gen X and even earlier. Autism wasn't truly understood, and chances are if you had it, it took you a long time to fumble across a diagnosis.

I came out of my own confused beginnings brimming with stories, but few useful stories escaped from this nebula. All I knew was that I wanted to be a writer, and I could not be swayed from this goal.

It turns out many autistic people have a hyperfixation, and telling stories was mine.

There was writing advice around, groups where you could meet with other aspiring writers and workshop your pieces, but nothing felt right. I met many fine people who guided my writing journey, but I didn't truly feel like I belonged at these tables.

Through sheer stubbornness and a healthy dose of luck, I managed to gain professional publication and achieved various accolades. I went on to teach writing workshops, mostly wanting to help people avoid my missteps. When I noticed that a large segment of these groups contained people with autism (you get a pretty good radar for others who are neurospicy!) the idea for Spectrum Writing was born.

A writing group designed for autistic people. Workshops that are actually fun and broken up to serve everyone, no matter how many spoons you have that day. A place where you could go off on a thousand tangents and not be judged. So, so many fidget toys.

In this book, Spectrum Writing is proud to provide a selection of professionally crafted stories from our writers, who have addressed the brief ably. They have written pieces around their special interests, whatever they are, with the end result being a great showcase of their skills.

The common thread I found with the accepted pieces is passion and sheer imagination. When doing something it really wants to do, nothing can hold back an autistic brain!

I could not be prouder of our Spectrum Writers, and these inspiring young writers have given me far more than I could ever hope to give. I hope this book is the beginning of many brilliant careers, and I cannot wait to see what they do next!

Jason Fischer
CEO and Founder
Spectrum Writing

Vesperian

James Stothard

Louren was a nation infamous for a great many reasons; whether that be its Obsidian Circle, who used magic forbidden by all others, or its Undying Legion whose soldiers endured all so long they have the will to live, or the shadowy intelligence networks of the Hidden Eye. But most infamous of all was their lord and master—Vesperian, the Undying Lord of Blackflame. He was the outcast-turned-emperor, who had struggled through a thousand trials to become the ruler of that most ominous of nations.

Many whispered about what visage lay under his armour of black-with-gold, what occult secrets were behind his mysterious powers, and how his unbreakable armaments came to be. But all such whispers had been hushed by the Battle of Soleia Castle, a brutal pyrrhic victory for Louren against its oldest rival as the Burning Prince finally met his end at Vesperian's hand after all others had been reduced to less than ash.

The Royal Family of Soleia was enraged that the Undying yet lived, while their most dreaded warrior had perished, the most galling grievance in centuries of conflict. Though they had kept the Prince bound in chains for fear of his strength, he was family still. And thus did they swear vengeance, deep and true, against the Undying Lord. They would kill the unkillable, no matter how long it took or how extreme the measures were required.

The sorcerer-smiths of Soleia pored over tomes of forbidden knowledge captured from Louren bought from other nations, or unsealed from old vaults in the hopes of finally devising something that might end their most hated foe. They had discovered that he was Undying for his body and mind were dead, kept animate by the invincible spirit and the primordial Abyss, the only success amongst a mountain of corpses. But such powers were not infallible, and they sought to create something which might force him into the stillness of death.

Though they worked in secrecy, the Hidden Eye of Louren reached many shadowy corners; and so word reached in his sable hall of a true attempt upon his life. He set out that night on his lonesome, for his armies had yet to recover. Covered in a ragged cloak so that none would know him as Lord, he ventured through the mountains to the hidden place where the sorcerers toiled, far from any civilization, approaching as a simple wanderer.

The guards, junior forces who had been far from the fateful battle, shouted warnings at the dirtied vagrant who had no doubt lost their way so far from the roads. Shouts continued and weapons were drawn as the wanderer continued with a purposeful stride. A final warning, then arrows were fired, only for them to bounce off the armour of the stranger as they continued, unfazed, toward the gate. In a single motion, they drew their sword and shattered the stone doors with one strike.

Rubble flew across the yard, alarms set off, and troops moved to stop the intruder before they could make it deeper into the compound proper. The intruder made no haste, simply walking as a platoon of soldiers formed before them with a wall of heavy shields and thrusting spears. The soldiers moved as one and struck forth with two dozen thrusts all in unison, but the intruder simply swung once to shatter their spears, twice to rend their shields, and a third to end their lives.

Stepping over the broken bodies, Vesperian approached the inner gate that led underground, where the sorcerers toiled. It was sealed shut with ensorcelled iron, such that none save a chosen few could hope to open it, but Vesperian knew another way. He cast aside any pretense of disguise as Blackflame surged forth from his body, its entropic power disintegrating his cloak, revealing his black-with-gold armour in full, a sight that all Soleia had learned to fear. He readied his blade and the dark flames swirled and billowed around it as he rent apart the doors, each swing tearing more and more until he had sundered them apart enough to fit through. Not one year ago, he would have simply destroyed it in a single blow, but he still hadn't recovered from his battle with the Prince.

Even so, there was work to do. Vesperian stepped into the compound proper and recognised the sigils carved on the walls—the arts of Obsidian Circle, meant to bind the Abyss into service. Concerning, both that they had such things at all, and that they sought to bind instead of destroy as most of Soleia would. Down dark stone stairs, he entered a chamber filled with statues of armoured warriors in battle positions, all facing away from the entrance.

Vesperian knew their purpose immediately, for he had seen this trick of the sorcerer-smiths many times before. Fearless war constructs lying in wait for an unsuspecting foe, a useful precaution against Abyssal horrors. So he struck first, shattering the nearest two in a single swing, and as predicted the rest stepped off their pedestals and charged him. Within a minute all had been reduced to shattered masonry, for few horrors could compare to the Undying Lord, the walking paradox whose existence was no longer of this world.

More stairs lead down, and the binding sigils that covered the walls grew more sophisticated, on the level expected of adepts. Worrying signs of progress already and there was yet deeper to go. As he reached the third chamber, and tore the door off its hinges, he entered what was certainly a workshop. Worktables were covered in projects from chains covered in intricate runework, nets of iridescent silver, great sarcophagi made of dark stone, and corpses of Abyssal horrors real enough to be dissected.

Having heard the commotion above sorcerer-smiths had gathered their most complete works and left in a hurry, leaving tools strewn about the room. With nothing to stop him, Vesperian moved through the room, eyeing their work as he went. And thus, could not help but notice that much of it was broken, as sarcophagus fragments lay in piles, net threads snapped, and more. Despite their progress, their work was insufficient for their task.

The next door was carved of dark stone like the walls, covered in sigil as well, but proved no match for the full momentum of an overhead strike by a sprinting armoured demigod. As the great stone door fell before him, he saw the sorcerer-smiths, sun-yellow uniforms recognisable anywhere, on the far side of a ritual chamber. All ten of their faces twisted in fear as they realised who stood before them, each clutching their most advanced creations protectively.

He bounded forward immediately, sped along by jets of Blackfire, singling out the closest sorcerer. But they were quick-thinking and had already reached for their Abyssal sarcophagus, unleashing the thing sealed inside. In the instant they did so a silhouette-black thing of impenetrable darkness simply appeared between them. Vesperian's blade struck this darkness-thing and space twisted into knots, flinging him into the wall. In this moment of distraction, the sorcerer-smiths made their escape further down, to prepare more thoroughly. Vesperian recovered swiftly and prepared his battle stance to consider his foe. A creature of the Abyss for certain, an alien thing dredged from beyond by sorcerous experiments, by this very room no doubt.

The darkness-thing was indescribable for the simple reason that Vesperian had no idea what he was truly looking at; it was simply a shape of utter blackness, from which only its blurred outline could be discerned. Its movements, if you could call them such, were sudden and erratic as thorn-like geometric extrusions simply appeared and disappeared from a central mass. With a sweeping gesture, a wave of Blackflame covered the darkness-thing to no effect; it didn't even seem to realise it had been attacked. An undying being much like himself then, no amount of force could stop it. Thus more esoteric means must be used.

Vesperian focused himself as he called upon his connection to the Abyss, and channelled its otherworldly power time-warped through himself. Energies from beyond enveloped his body and then his blade, starting as monochrome but growing more and more colourful and vibrant and chaotic as more power coalesced. Colours beyond the world shined, space bent around them, and time-warped erratically. The darkness-thing sensed what was occurring and its extrusions branched and multiplied in a vain attempt to escape. As reality buckled under the strain, Vesperian swung and carved open a great rift in the universe where the darkness-thing was, and sent it back to the maddening depths of the Abyss.

The colours vanished and Vesperian collapsed to his knees as the connection between body and spirit wavered. His power stemmed from the Abyss, and drawing too deeply upon it was like exhaustion, as its paradoxical power allowed him to remain active despite his deathly nature. A moment passed and he got up, for as nice as rest would be, he had to keep going; there was yet more to do, more secrets to find, and more heights to reach, and he yet had the strength to see it through.

The way forward was clear, and Vesperian knew they were preparing for his attack, and so prepared something of his own. The Blackflame gathered around his body, all of it that he could muster in his weakened state, surging in intensity but remaining contained as he approached the door. His every step reduced stone to dust, and then to less than that, as he walked. At the door, he readied himself as he unleashed the totality of his gathered power, releasing a torrent of light-devouring flame as he tore through the dark stone at superhuman speeds.

An explosion of dark fire engulfed the room, but the sorcerers had been prepared. They had taken no chances, each stood protected from the blast by a dozen layers of arcane shielding, armed with their most successful creations, and well-learned in the ways of their foe. Even as the first three layers were obliterated in the initial blast, the remaining stood strong. But it would only be a matter of time until the dark fire unmade the rest, and then they would be helpless against the Undying Lord and their mission would be for naught. And so they held strong even as Vesperian's mere passing sent them soaring into the walls with enough force to shatter another shield layer.

Now face-to-face with his quarry, Vesperian knew exactly what they were planning with a glance. Force him into stillness and seal him away, such that he might never trouble Soleia again. Clever enough, but they would have to catch him first, and he had no intent of slowing down. As Vesperian hit the far wall, cracking stone, three sorcerers cast out golden chains that moved through the air by their makers will, each reaching for a separate limb. Before they could reach him, Vesperian was already soaring off in another blast of Blackflame, hurtling toward the most ill-prepared sorcerer.

Panicking, they cast a silver net out, but it was already too late. Vesperian's blinding speed, roaring flames, and sword edge tore through their already-faltering protections. They cut through with little resistance, their bodies disintegrating from the Blackflame. Still moving faster than most could follow, Vesperian kicked off the wall of the chamber with another room-shaking blast. He hurled himself at the next sorcerer, who dived out of the way, casting out dozens of binding talismans, dimming the Blackflame as they found purchase upon Vesperian.

But it was not enough to save them as Vesperian struck again, slower this time, and they died with his sword through their heart. But now the sorcerers were no longer on the backfoot as chains soared through the air and damaged shielding was restored. But one chain-wielder had left themselves open, thus Vesperian leapt upon them with another surge of fire. A flurry of blows shattered their protections but cost him precious time, and as he drove the blade into their neck, he felt their chain bind his legs. As blood poured forth, the sorcerer smiled triumphantly as they died. Vesperian lunged again at the closest but was bound such his movements were unwieldy, and only managed to injure them before another chain caught his arm, and then the third.

Now vulnerable, Vesperian was covered in every form of binding the sorcerers had devised; rune-carved chains, sacred nets, cursed talismans, and more he couldn't recognise. Though he railed against it, thrashing with inhuman force and surging dark flames, he could hear the rumbling of heavy stone as the sorcerers prepared his sarcophagus. He felt himself move, and then a great thud of slamming stone around him.

In an instant, all went silent. His struggling ceased, the flames extinguished, and even thinking became difficult. The sorcerers outside took no chances as they covered the sarcophagus in everything they had left, and with no sign of movement, they knew it had worked. Within a day they had set off with the tomb in tow, toward the Soleian capital. From there the royal family saw to it, taking it to the deepest dungeons where the Burning Prince had once dwelled and collapsed the whole area on top of it, burying the Undying Lord underneath countless tons of stone. The royals claimed victory, Louren wailed, and their war continued.

But the sorcerers had miscalculated, for their work was to counter the Abyss, and that was but one part of Vesperian. Even in utter darkness, bound in chains, his powers dimmed and sealed by a dozen forms of sorcery, his spirit remained unbroken. And so as the earth crashed around him did a single finger twitch, igniting a small flame no larger than a candle, and ever so slowly started to wear away at the chains.

Time lost all meaning. How long had it taken for the small flame to finally wear down the first chain link? Days? Months? Years? He had no way of knowing and so he kept at it, slowly but surely. One by one, piece by piece, each chain was undone and so he could once again move, however slightly. Next the nets and their threads snapped and withered until he felt his candle flame swell to a brazier. The flames were turned upon the talismans, whose curses could only hold so long against metaphysical fire.

When the last one finally fell away, Vesperian could freely move once more—as much as one could inside a greatstone sarcophagus, and half buried in dust. And so Vesperian turned to his next obstacle, the sarcophagus itself. There was not enough room for his sword to be used, and so he used the only other method available. He began to punch the sarcophagus lid. Again and again, each infused with all the Blackflame he could muster. Through all this time, the power of the sarcophagus had remained intact, and to move with strength, speed, and precision required him to fight through its influence each and every time.

He kept hammering away, striking the same spot over and over. He couldn't tell if he was making progress or not, for Blackflame gave off no light, but he was Undying by his invincible spirit. And so he simply kept going. Sometimes his mind wandered, wondering how long it had been, and what could await him outside. Was Louren still standing? What of Soleia? But each time he set those thoughts aside and focused on the task at hand. To ponder such things would only lead to delusion and disappointment, and then he would simply have to accept whatever awaited him.

And so he continued, hammering away again and again until one day he heard a crack as his latest blow struck true and, for the first time in ages, he felt a sliver of his old power stir within him. He mustered up that sliver and struck again, his fist going into the stone itself and spreading cracks that caused chunks of stone to fall from the sarcophagus. And he felt more of his power rising to his will, and Vesperian reached for his sword that had been at his side all this time, focused all of his might, and struck one final time.

For miles around, the earth shook as a wave of otherworldly energies tore through countless tons of stone. A great and terrible pillar of black fire burst forth from the ground, soaring higher until it reached the clouds before dissipating as suddenly as it had come, leaving only a great chasm in its wake. And amidst the clouds, Vesperian approached the apex of his ascent. Gazing out at the sky he hadn't seen in so long, he allowed himself a moment of peace to take in the serenity of a clear blue sky.

The moment passed and, as he began to fall, Vesperian's mind moved on to more pressing matters. He had no fear of falling, being more than durable enough to survive terminal velocity unharmed, but it was what awaited below him that concerned him. Even at this distance he recognised Soleian architecture, but knew something was off. He hit the ground with a stone-shattering crash and looked up to see that the whole city was in ruins, and clearly had been for many years. Centuries, even.

The Soleia he knew was long gone, likely violently if the damage were anything to go by. Louren had surely been undone by external foes or internal tensions or had changed beyond recognition without him. He was alone in the world, any knowledge of him relegated to legends. He had no idea what to do now.

So Vesperian picked a random direction and started walking. He was Undying, he would find something to do sooner or later.

The End.

Impending Fear

Jasmin Punger-Glass

I stand here waiting
For what, I do not know
A sense of doom encompasses me
My fear begins to grow
Like storm clouds on the horizon
Dark and bruised and menacing
My thoughts grow dark and sinister
I cannot stop them entering
Just as a cloud releases
My tears build, and begin to fall
Uncontrollable, as is nature's way
I no longer stand tall
I gasp for breath between each sob
My fear has been realised
Uncontrolled I fall apart
I reach for hope, idealised

Karal Isle

Callum Henry-Edwards

Hello! You found my journal if you're reading this! Good job! Yippee! Anyway, if you want to know what I put in here, I actually don't know, because I haven't written it yet. This is the start of the book, dummy. Tomorrow, we leave for the Karal Isle (and stop in Cabo Verde for supplies), and I'm hoping to document the species I find there. Oh, I'm Will; I just remembered that I had forgotten to say that. I will be documenting my journey to the Isles day by day.

Day one: Today was the day we set off from port. I bid farewell to my sister and sailed away into the great unknown. I snuck my tarot deck on board. I enjoy having it with me—it makes me feel safe and reminds me of my mother. Other than that, it's been very peaceful on the first day. I assume—*hope*—it will be the same for the rest of the journey.

Day two: Nothing of note happened today. It's very different being out at sea, rather than back in Britain.

Day three: There's a small school of fish swimming beneath the ship, I can't quite make out the species. Maybe tuna?

Day four: I saw a whale today, it was blue. I like whales. I'm bored of the crackers and dried meat.

Day seven: We finally arrived in Cabo Verde. I love being able to have fruit again.

Day eight: Still in Cabo Verde.

Day nine: I'm out at sea again.

Day nine: We've been out on the open ocean for quite some time now, I'm getting anxious. I've never been at sea for this long.

Day eleven: I just realised I wrote day nine twice, rather than ten. . . Nothing interesting happened today.

Day twelve: Unfortunately, something. . . interesting happened today—a storm, to be specific. We've been blown off course significantly. While the storm was raging, I saw. . . something, some great monster from the depths. It was vaguely serpentine, and it must've been at least the size of a whale. It had beautiful blue scales with orange spikes. I could barely see its head beneath the water, but I could see its horns and its bright glowing white eyes.

When the storm ended, I found a small locket on the deck. It's gold and intricately engraved with flowers. I couldn't manage to get it to open; it's got a small keyhole on the side. Really wish I had the key.

Last night, I had a terrible nightmare, a nightmare filled with monsters and beasts. I saw four glowing eyes—four terrible, glowing eyes. I awoke in a cold sweat. I found one of my tarot cards on the floor; The Tower—the card that represents disaster, and chaos.

So, not good signs for the rest of this journey.

Day thirteen: I *hate* crackers. I want fruit. We ran out two days ago.

Day fourteen: I can see some clouds near the horizon; they're surrounded by normal clouds, but these are... *different*. They're glossier than the ones around them and less fluffy—when I zoom in on them with my spyglass, I swear I can see eyes and tendrils. Maybe I shouldn't have gone on this journey.

The clouds took someone.

Day fifteen: The crew and I fished something up from the depths today. We were hoping to catch something to eat, so we could finally stop eating these crackers, even just for a day. But instead, we found this odd stopwatch; it looks to be much the same design as the locket. I don't know how this got down there, nor do I know how the locket got on board.

Day sixteen: Last night I was awoken by a loud noise from one of the cabins. I walked out onto the fog-covered deck on my way to see what had happened. I saw the creature's neck spooled out on the deck like rope, slinking onto the ship from the depths below. The screaming of my crewmates echoed out, dampened by the fog. A wet thud reverberated from the dark hallways of the cabin, and the creature snaked out into the open silently. Its sharp white teeth glimmered in the moonlight, and its wide forehead glowed dimly, growing brighter every moment. And then it sang with a hauntingly beautiful voice. I was enthralled by its brilliant display. Despite the siren call of the wyrm, Bernard took the initiative and shot the wyrm in its slimy neck with our harpoon cannon. We all had tea afterward, and I got given a blanket.

It's a nice blanket.

Day seventeen: We're here! I forgot how much I love the land. It's very warm here though—which is bad. I've been to Spain before, and this is somehow worse. It's like Spain, without the *s*. I've found some interesting shrubs and ferns growing near the beach, as well as some almost frighteningly large crabs. They must be at least a metre across. The crabs appear to be a new species, and thus I name this new species: The Colossal Sand Crab. They're rather bizarre critters, but I'm quite fond of them. They seem to be much smarter than most crustaceans too, sharing fish they've caught amongst themselves. I'm not sure how exactly they hunt, but due to their slow speed, I presume they are ambush predators, lying in wait for their meal.

We're staying on the ship tonight. Thankfully, Bernard and some of the others are setting up camp in a nice clearing on the land. It's exciting being here, so many new sights and discoveries to make.

I saw a thing again, in a dream, it was different this time. I saw a woman, with flowing green hair, speckled with leaves and flowers. She had legs and hooves like that of a deer, horns like that of a ram, and eyes with beautiful golden irises surrounded by black sclera. She held a blue jay in one of her long-clawed hands, and then I woke. I found another card from my deck removed; the empress—a card representing femininity and the creation of life. I wonder if these dreams will continue.

Day eighteen: I've just found out this morning that during my sleep, my hair grew seven centimetres. This isn't normal; it's past my chin now. I've decided not to cut it—I think it looks nice. The camp is fully set up now, and we're beginning to move in. It's all just simple wooden housing, but I think it'll do nicely. In other news, we've found our second new animal on the island; it's this weird messed-up little guy that keeps screaming at me. I have absolutely no clue what this is, or if it's an invertebrate or vertebrate. I honestly can't tell what to make of it. I've dubbed it. Bernard told me to call it Boingo after his favourite clown back in his hometown in New Jersey. I didn't argue with him about it because it's not like I had a better name for it. It unfortunately skedaddled away into the shrubbery while we were discussing its enormous yellow eyes, so we weren't able to dissect it.

Not too much else happened today, Bernard had an encounter with a snake, but unfortunately, it's an already documented species.

I'm writing this at three in the morning. Gerald (he's one of the ship's hands) came running out of the woods at around nine in the evening, screaming before collapsing onto the grass. Despite his heart still beating in his chest, and his breathing continuing, there was no life in his eyes, and his face remained petrified with fear. An hour later, Gerald awoke with no memory of the events.

Day nineteen: I've found something fascinating; a human-sized clay sculpture just outside the campsite. It's wearing a metal mask, with a wide toothy grin. I believe that the mask is composed of bronze, but I am unsure. Quite disturbingly, there appear to be bones sticking out of the arm stump. There are no clues as to how it got there. Written on its abdomen is text written in—as far as I know—an unknown script. Just under the text, there are what I believe to be two numbers written next to each other, with a line between them. Due to all this information, I believe this to be a sort of bizarre effigy of a deceased individual. Who this could be—or the culture of origin it is from—I have no idea. I've decided to name it the "Clay Effigy."

IT ATTACKED ME IT MOVED I T M O V E D IT MOVED IT MOVED IT MOVED

I'm sorry about that; I had a panic attack last night. I was getting ready for bed when I heard the rapid rustling of grass and hard footfalls approaching the campsite, it must have been ten steps a second. It occasionally fell silent, before starting once more. I looked outside my tent, and the steps began anew. I shot my gaze left and saw the clay effigy with its open palm mere inches from my neck.

It had stopped in its tracks the second I saw it. I blinked once and its hand wrapped around my throat tightly. I stared into its cold metal eyes as it stared back. I stared at the monster for what felt like forever, my eyes red with pain. Blood poured from the sculpture's mouth. I had to blink. A sat an eternity, for a long, agonising moment, when Bernard cut through the sculpture's arm with an axe. The hand was still tightly wrapped around my neck. Bernard kept hacking at the effigy, chunks of clay flying in several directions. Eventually, the statue was reduced to nothing but rubble, bone, and its mask. I haven't seen any of the chunks move, and as far as I know, the bones are normal human bones.

I had another dream, it showed me a place; a desert of black sand, and clouds that reminded oneself of the Milky Way. Three figures sat in a building of black sandstone playing cards; the first, an all spindly man with a wide and sharp toothy grin, like a shark's. His eyes were made from clocks, ticking slowly along, and his blue hair and suit shone brilliant cyan light off himself. It was nearly impossible to make out any emotions from him while he looked at his hand of cards.

The second was a short woman, dressed in clothing like a jester, a bit of her pink hair poking out from under her hat. She looked at the cards in her hand smugly, clearly believing that she was to win the game next turn.

The third woman was more pale than snow and had bright yellow and purple irises, surrounded by black sclera. Two long pointed horns sat atop her head, poking through her large witch hat. Her tail fidgeted idly with a rock while she inspected her cards deep in thought. I saw their cards:

The spindly man held Temperance.

The short jester woman held The Fool.

And the demonic horned woman held The Magician.

Day twenty: I went out for a bit of an exploration today! It feels good to be out in nature again. Actually found a large mammal today. It looks like an elephant but with smaller ears. Unfortunately, there isn't much to say about them; they're fairly territorial and fairly normal. I can't get close enough to the beasts to study them, but it is amazing to find elephants outside of Africa. I also found an armadillo hiding in some grass, but the species isn't new.

I saw the effigy's mask in a dream. Its bronze mask smiled at me, malice in its hollow eyes. The mask itself was many times the size of Big Ben. Its mask connected to a gargantuan machine, stretching on and curving into the shape of a head unfathomably far. Cogs and gears on the outskirts of its body laid dormant, but clicking and turning echoed out from deep within.

The head of course connected to a body, buried beneath the mountains around it. Plant life engulfed the machine, stretching deep into the clockwork. When I awoke, I found the effigy's mask nearby, with the tarot card for the Wheel of Fortune beneath it.

Day twenty-one: Hey, so, big news, there's more effigies, hundreds more. Bernard and I found them out in a forest, standing immobile, each holding its pose perfectly. Luckily for us, they seem to be completely unable to move in the day, as they haven't attacked us. We were daring enough to make passage through the woodlands, and we were rewarded for it. As it turns out, we're not the only sentient creatures living here. First, I'll give some background; on the other end of the forest are grand mountains, taller than the highest buildings in London. Little caves dot the mountains, and inside the caves is the creature that I want to talk about. I've made friends with these lovely little crustaceous creatures living in these caverns. I can't speak their language, and they can't speak mine, but we've managed to communicate quite effectively with hand gestures and with objects.

The Crabfolk—which is what I'm calling them—are a very friendly species, sharing a close resemblance to, well, crabs—especially the gargantuan sand crab. Initially, they threatened me with spears while walking around me sideways, but with some gifts of rations, we managed to convince them we were friendly. Despite being crustaceans, they have a few major differences; they have a body structure uncannily similar to humans, possessing a definable head and torso. Their lower body reminds me more of an insect rather than a crab, being elongated like the abdomen of an ant. They have six limbs on their lower body, and four on their upper body acting as arms—two of their four arms being claws. They are the same shade of deep wooden brown as the sand crabs. They have fairly rudimentary wool clothing.

They're still odd, but I don't find them to be as barbaric as some of my companions seem to believe they are. Bernard thinks they're savages. We barely made it back to camp before dark, and we've moved ourselves onto the ship and raised the plank now that we know about the effigies.

Day twenty-two: I heard scratching all through the night, but the good news is that the clay effigies couldn't get on the ship. When we left the ship, we saw them all standing, completely motionless at the side of the ship. While the rest of the crew worked on the new reinforced campsite, I set off to visit the Crabfolk. When I arrived, I immediately set to studying them and their culture. In doing so, I have discovered that they have domesticated a species of sheep, which I am dubbing the four-horned sheep—I wonder if you can guess how many horns they have!

One specific Crabfolk stood out to me; it was taller than the other Crabfolk, and its shell was a muted grey colour. Coral-like protrusions stuck out from its head, and it wore a dark black cloak over its body. At midday, a group of Crabfolk—including the grey one—began trekking up a small mountain. It took around two hours for us to reach the peak, and on the way, I picked up a rock—this is important I swear—where an altar had been built from the stone of the mountain.

The Crabfolk then began worshipping together on the peak of the mountain, singing strange little hymns together in an utterly incomprehensible language. It was oddly beautiful. The grey crab placed a piece of uncut opalite onto the altar, and blue smoke poured from the stone; the smoke's hue shifted to a deep purple, and I heard distant and sinister cackling. And then I passed out and woke up in my cabin.

I think I might've hallucinated the whole thing, but. . . I still have the rock.

Day twenty-three: The crew insisted that I stay in my tent today; they say that I look pale, but I feel fine. I feel good. I feel fantastic. They keep saying I'm delirious, and I'm making bad decisions.

They're wrong. I've discovered a new species today, and I have absolutely no clue what it is. It looks like a combination of an echidna and an anteater. It's a fairly dull orange colour, and about the size of a foxhound, but much weightier. I've observed it sniffing around in the soil eating small bugs, and even catching and eating a rodent of some kind. I've named it the Snoovel because I don't care anymore. I love being outdoors. Nature is beautiful. I must hold the locket it's mine no one else can have it *its mine*.

BRONZEFACE ORDERS THEE TO GIFT THE WATCH TO ME

THE CRABS ARE NOT MY KIN

ASSOCIATE WITH THEM NOT

ASSOCIATE NOT WITH THE KIN OF LILITH

FOUL MAGICIAN

A HARECOP SHE BE

A MUCK-SPOUT SHE BE

I've just woken up, I didn't write that. I'm going to keep meeting with the Crabfolk.

Day twenty-four: Today, I'm out with the Crabfolk once more—sorry Bronze Face. I'm studying their rituals. They have prepared me a cloak. I adore their kindness. They have allowed me to explore their home. They have masks of clay effigies hung up, but based on what I now know, I'd bet that these are the masks of slain effigies. The Crabfolk have gifted me their local cuisine, a soup, filled with root vegetables and fish. I've decided to stay with the Crabfolk tonight.

Day twenty-five: I've done a small religious ritual with the Crabfolk. They used the locket as a component and figured out what I could not. They used the big hand of the watch as the key.

What amazes me most is that they didn't have to discover this. They knew. They already knew. As soon as the locket was opened, I grasped my head in agony. My head felt like it was splitting in half until my eyes were open. I saw everything. I saw space, saw stars be born and die, I saw. . . Empires rise and fall. . . and then I fell with them.

Hi Will!! Great job!!! You're so close to finishing what I need you to do! SO CLOSE!!!

I just

Need

That

SOUL

You have

In fact, I'll prepare you a contract.

I get your SOUL

And YOU

Get to see your dear mother again

Does that sound

Good?

Will?

What?

I'm offering you a deal for your SOUL what don't you get

What do you mean I get to see my mother again? She's alive back in Wales.

Oh shit, really?

Yeah.

Damn, really thought she died based on the way you wrote about her

No, I just miss her.

Okay new deal

I make you a GOD

And you gimme your SOUL

Good deal?

Who is this?

Lilith, Goddess of Monsters and Stuff

Okay, just sign here:

Oh, I don't remember my surname.

YOU FORGOT YOUR SURNAME????

I think it's the stuff I did with the opalite.

Oh my lord, ok, fine, new surname.

Can't think of one. Also, will this be legally binding? How do contracts with eldritch deities work?

They just do

Fair enough.

Okay, how about wisp??

Get it?

Because you're Will

Will Wisp

Will O'Wisp

I'm funny

Yeah, okay.

Sign:

William Wisp.

THEN

IT'S

A

DEAL

SMILING AT STRANGERS

CATHERINE MORGAN

In retail, there is a phrase: *The customer is always right*. There is actually a second, lesser-known part to that phrase: *Because every customer has a story*.

Monday

Click, whir, click! We're pricing books together with the pricing gun. *Click, whir, click!* The asphalt footpath outside is starting to melt in the heat. *Click, whir, click!* Mystery novel. Cookbook. Poetry. History. Field guide to birds. Sci-fi novel. *Click whir, click!* What's your favourite novel?

You ask them because you're curious. Her red lipstick looks garish and has melted a little in the summer heat. She tells me, so serious that your heart becomes a stone when you hear it—

She doesn't believe in books, she doesn't believe in stories. If it's not real, it's not worth it.

Click, whir, wait—what? You try to imagine a world without stories, and you imagine no world at all. You put the pricing gun down and walk away before you put a price tag on her head. A world with no space for stories is a world you don't want to see. The day there stops being stories is the day we will stop thriving. You promise yourself you will pick up a pen, in defiance of red lipstick and not believing in stories, to write this one.

Tuesday

A gaggle of lip gloss and gossip have populated the changing rooms for some time. They try on green, blue, and black dresses—denim jackets and velvet pants. One girl in the group is standing apart, not just a few feet, but miles away. Her gaze falls downwards, avoiding the mirror. Until one of the others says— you should try this on, go on, try this on. It's gorgeous. It's gorgeous, sure. It's also two sizes too small. Barely contained snickers. Even after the footsteps leave, even after the gaggle of girls recedes. . . you can stand in the changing rooms and feel the exact spot she wanted the world to swallow her up. When you step on it, the carpet gives a little.

Wednesday

The coat hangers are tangled up again. You'll stay back and sort out it. Nowhere better to be. After the loud one and the tattooed one have left, it's just you and the coat hangers. Your fingers are nimble. Coat hangers hang. The fans hum the air heavy, holding its breath, waiting for bad news. Everything is in order. In the break room, you pour yourself an orange cordial. It's unpleasant and tepid. You spot a fly drifting in the cup, drowning a sweet, sticky death. You worry you might fall in too. When was the last time you swam?

Thursday

The clothes are being sorted into piles: Good enough. Not good enough.

A small price to pay for the clothes that come looking for a new life, puppies to the pound, abandoned. There's a jacket with a tiny stain. It has to go. If it's not perfect, it's not good enough. Yet here is where the clothes come when there's nowhere else to go, where they seek refuge for another life beyond their first. What about the clothes that aren't good enough? Not good enough for the public to see, to be worn in the world. The rejects, the unwearable. The unseeable. If you're not perfect, you won't make the cut. Clothes surround us and most sit in the hollow space of the bin, no longer of use to the world. You sort me into the correct pile. Not good enough. She gives me that look and with a roll of her eyes sorts me back into the correct pile, in her opinion: Good enough.

Friday

She barges in, hair neat, tied back, held together. Outwardly composed, two large plastic bags in tow.

Won't be needing these anymore—tight smile. She stares intently at the crockery. Clears throat. Eyes become pools. Won't be needing these anymore—

Stands there, her hands locked on the black bundles. The shop shelves groan under the weight of all they hold. The thin plastic makes no sound as she holds them up mid-air. Suspended. You take out your film camera and this moment exists in a gallery somewhere rich in sepia. You call it: The Art of Letting Go.

You'll use the key to lock up the shop. Heave a deep breath through your tired lungs. The models in the windows are looking sad, but at least they have a roof over their heads and clothes on their backs. You'll be back tomorrow. You'll meet more customers, sell more clothes, and hear more stories. You'll head home, fall asleep, and take your wings to fly somewhere where they believe in stories.

Destiny's Bible of Beasts and Beauties

Kade Bailey

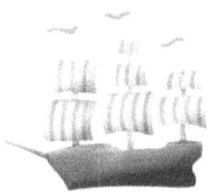

PART I:

The Mirror Dragon

Appearance:

The Mirror Dragon is a majestic creature with wings that reflect the colours of the rainbow, creating a glorious and mesmerising sight. Its reflective wings glisten with the entire spectrum of colours, making it a breathtaking spectacle to behold.

Habitat and Behaviour:

The Mirror Dragon can manipulate light, creating blinding displays that can disorient or captivate anyone who happens to look their way. It is known to inhabit areas with ample sunlight, utilising its control over light to create stunning visual displays to deter predators. The dragon's ability to trap individuals in their illusions adds an element of danger to its presence.

Ecological Impact:

The Mirror Dragon's ability to manipulate light and create dazzling displays can have a significant impact on its ecosystem. It may influence the behaviour of other creatures in its habitat, and potentially alter the balance of predator-prey dynamics. The blinding displays it creates may also serve as a defence mechanism, affecting the behaviour of other species within its environment.

Encounters and Legends:

Encounters with the Mirror Dragon are rare and often shrouded in mystery and awe. Its captivating displays and ability to manipulate light have given rise to numerous legends and tales. Stories of individuals being entranced or ensnared by the dragon's illusions have contributed to its enigmatic reputation, making it a figure of both fascination and caution in folklore and mythology.

The Coral Behemoth

Appearance:

The Coral Behemoth is a colossal creature. It is reminiscent of a living reef sitting atop something akin to the Norse mythology Kraken, covered in an array of vibrant and razor-sharp coral formations. Its size and slow-moving nature give it a daunting presence, making it an incredible sight to behold.

Habitat and Behaviour:

This creature is typically found in coral-rich environments, such as vibrant coral reefs and underwater caverns. Its ability to blend in with the surrounding coral formations makes it challenging for prey and predators alike to detect its presence until it's too late. The Coral Behemoth moves with a deliberate and quickened pace, seemingly in sync with the gentle swaying of the coral around it. Its movements are calculated, allowing it to conserve energy while remaining a formidable force in its environment.

Camouflage:

The creature's ability to blend seamlessly with the natural coral formations serves as both a defensive mechanism and a hunting strategy. Unsuspecting prey may mistake it for part of the reef, only realising their mistake when they are within striking distance of the creature's razor-sharp coral adornments.

Ecological Impact:

The presence of the Coral Behemoth has a significant impact on its ecosystem. Its slow movements create microhabitats for smaller marine life, providing shelter and opportunities for symbiotic relationships. Additionally, the creature's feeding habits and interactions with the surrounding environment contribute to the shaping of the underwater landscape, further solidifying its role as a vital species within its habitat.

Encounters and Legends:

Stories and legends among seafaring communities speak of awe-inspiring encounters with the Coral Behemoth. Some tales depict it as a guardian of the reefs, while others warn of its formidable nature, urging caution to those who venture into its domain.

The Blazing Bear:

Appearance:

The Blazing Bear is a mythical creature that captivates the imagination with its fiery fur, molten lava, and extraordinary abilities. Resembling a bear, it is adorned with fiery fur that engulfs its entire body, creating a mesmerising spectacle. The molten lava flowing through its veins adds to its otherworldly appearance, giving it an aura of power and intensity.

Flame:

With the ability to breathe streams of scorching fire, the Blazing Bear becomes a living embodiment of destruction and heat. Its flames can engulf its surroundings, leaving a trail of devastation in its wake. This unique ability sets it apart from other mystical creatures and makes it a formidable force to be reckoned with.

Earth:

In addition to its mastery of fire, the Blazing Bear possesses the remarkable power to manipulate the earth itself. With a single swipe of its powerful paws, the ground cracks and shifts beneath its weight. This ability allows the Blazing Bear to create fissures in the earth, altering the landscape to its advantage. It can reshape the terrain, making it a force of both destruction and creation.

Destructive capabilities

The presence of the Blazing Bear in its environment can have major ecological impacts. Its ability to manipulate the earth and unleash scorching fire affects the local ecosystem and landscape. The changes it brings can disrupt the natural balance and have far-reaching consequences for the plants, animals, and other creatures that inhabit the area.

Encounters and legends:

Legends and tales have been woven around the Blazing Bear, adding to its mystique and significance. Stories of encounters with other mythical creatures and their role as a guardian of the natural world have been passed down through generations. The Blazing Bear symbolizes the raw power of nature and serves as a reminder of the delicate balance between destruction and creation.

Beneath the David

Jason Fischer

They found it in Florence during repairs.
The atrium around the David badly damaged.
Foot traffic, the weight of obsession
Tiles scraped bare around the perfection of A Man
The workers discovered a chamber beneath.
Authorities moved fast, shoring up that priceless stone
But curiosity digs.
Torchlight showed another statue,
A child of soft confusion
Flat stare, a weak smile to appease
Not a classical pose,
The stone unsure of how to hold itself.
All too aware of the contrapposto above it.
Unaware of itself as load-bearing.
Experts descended with harness and line
'A New Form Of Man!' they cried.
Only to find thousands down there, huddled

A forest of genius in the dark.
'How did you get here? When?'
No eye contact. The answer, atonal.
'We've always been here.'

WHaT YOU Can Learn ABOUT VISUAL STORYTELLING From a SINGLE SCene In ILLUMINATION'S SING 2

RaCHeL Bauer

Most people will look down upon *Illumination's Sing 2*. It's a kids movie, it's a jukebox musical, it's made by the Minion studio. But by doing so, they miss out on a diamond of a scene, a study in visual filmmaking and short film: Johnny's climactic scene. When I'm done, you will want to watch Sing 2. Or at least this scene.

Johnny, a young adult gorilla with a British accent, is arguably the deuteragonist of the Sing series. His characters are some of the most impactful, both emotionally and plot-wise. In the first movie, he must choose between loyalty to his gang leader father or his passion for performing. In the second movie, he must prove himself to a stubborn, and frankly abusive, dance instructor/choreographer, KlausKickenklober (yes, that is indeed his name). But you don't need to watch the whole movie to see the entire arc. You just need to watch one single three-and-a-half-minute scene.

The scene opens with an establishing shot, which is one of two wide shots in this scene. No surprises there. What is surprising is the actual scene: Johnny is wearing grey-blue armour, playing the piano, in front of a huge audience. There is a brief spotlight on the side which connects to the larger story of the movie, but it is irrelevant to both this essay and the scene. The piano and the song choice, 'Sky Full of Stars' by *Coldplay*, are incongruent with the stage setting. Shredded banners, rubble, a crashed spaceship, stars, and a hint of a nebula in the background. After the camera zooms in, Johnny looks up with a smile and bright eyes, and we see presumably his family and friends, as his father says 'That's my boy'. All of this together sets up who Johnny is; he's a lover, not a fighter. He is incongruent with this planet of war.

It also invites us to empathise with him. He has people that care about him and people that want to get in his way, which has great emotional effects on him. Watching someone express distinct and powerful emotions makes it easier to empathise. Aspiring actors, take note.

As Johnny sings the chorus, he looks up to a different location and does a double-take. There stands a proboscis monkey with a frown, flanked by two red-costumed characters who are enjoying the show. This is Klaus, and he appears to be the only one disapproving of the performance. Johnny then glances down, lowering his head. With just a double-take and a disapproving look, the conflict has been established. Additionally, the colour contrast and symbolism of the bright red costumes position him as a clear antagonist to the blue-costumed Johnny. This is visual storytelling efficiency at its peak. Zero words have been spoken between them.

Johnny scrunches his eyebrows and looks back to his support; a particular friend, Nooshy, is cheering him on. She is the focus of the frame because she will be important later. Johnny smiles and breaks into the last line of the chorus before stepping away from the piano to dance, as his supporters cheer him on and Klaus demands a red costume. It is obvious what Klaus is planning, building anticipation as the scene cuts away to the overarching antagonist of the film.

Now, without context, this cut-away scene can still be interesting. A limo careens through traffic and the pigdriver says they'll be at the theatre soon. Clearly, they're heading to Johnny. But why? Are they there to stop Johnny? To support him? Whoever it is, they're important. Now that we have a character that we care about, potential threats or supporters are notable and memorable. It also serves as a break, which allows Johnny's scene to skip ahead without wasting time going through every dance step.

Johnny is framed by the red and blue sides of the conflict until he is covered up in the centre frame by Klaus, who triumphantly grins. He is aware of the effect he has on Johnny, whose eyes widen. Johnny looks up to the de-costumed character, who shakes their head with palms spread. This was completely unplanned, and Johnny is unprepared. He glances around quickly, he fumbles with his jo staves (had to Google that one, plural of jo staff), and he crouches. Klaus grins, and Johnny's eyes narrow with uncertainty. When they begin the fight, Johnny's blocks are less direct, clumsy compared to Klaus' hits, which even cause Johnny to grunt as he is hit in the side and his supporters wince in sympathy (yes, even his thug father). The whole time, you see the fear in Johnny's eyes. Say what you will about *Illumination*, but they have pure talent in their animators to be able to pull off such nuanced body language in anthropomorphic animals.

We now get the second establishing shot, reminding us that this is supposed to be a performance, as Johnny is pushed to the side of the ring of fire. Wait, did I mention there was a ring of fire? Well, there is. The two move into the final position of the fight, standing entirely on their staves. With the larger context of the movie, this was the pose Johnny struggled the most to do, and Nooshy helped him achieve it. Klaus grimaces, Johnny's chin held high in effort. Even though he can do it, it's still not easy. But Klaus uses his staff to knock the staff from under Johnny, sending him to the floor. He jabs Johnny in the chest and says, 'You see, you will never be great, Johnny.' And Johnny simply lays his head back in defeat. Once again, we understand with just body language. In storytelling, this is the low point, the dark night of the soul where Johnny has given up. This moment is important because it emphasises the effect on Johnny. We see him at his lowest so we can empathise, so we understand what is to be gained and lost through Klaus' words, but also so that we can see him at his best as he rises from this defeat.

Nooshy begins drumming on the convenient empty barrel that she's been sitting on this whole time. Johnny smiles and begins singing an acapella version of the chorus. The melodic piano is gone, and with it went Johnny's gentleness. Both the red and blue sides begin rhythmically pounding their staves along with him. Klaus looks around in confusion as Johnny's movements become more aggressive. Klaus seems to be surprised, but once again goes to attack Johnny. But Johnny flips over him, his singing becoming more of a shout, a primal warcry. He flips around Klaus who struggles to hit him. As he finishes the chorus, the fight culminates with Johnny knocking Klaus' hat off, breaking his staff in two, and hitting his proboscis nose with a goofy *Looney Tunes* sound effect. Because this is for kids, after all. It was getting a bit dark. Never forget your target audience.

During the fight, Klaus struggles to hit Johnny. While this may just be for the story, to signify that Johnny is finally beating Klaus, there is potentially a deeper layer to this moment. Klaus is a choreographer. He works with carefully orchestrated moves, not instinct. This is the theme of the conflict; Johnny has superior raw talent and struggles to abide by Klaus' strict and narrow conception of dance. When playing by Klaus' rules, he loses. But when he takes back control and takes initiative, he thrives. As a neurodivergent individual, I find that incredibly inspiring Johnny has.

In the final frame of this scene, Johnny stares down at a stunned Klaus, his teeth bared. This is where the animalistic design adds to the story; Johnny has large lower fangs which enhances his animalistic intimidation. When designing characters, create them for the story, but also create the story from them. That is to say, let whoever the character is and their unique appearance influence the story just as much as it influences them.

Now let's talk about the general choices of this scene. First, the song. It not only matches the setting of a planet of war, with lines such as 'You're a sky full of stars' and 'Tear me apart, I don't care if you do', but it also encapsulates Johnny's interpersonal relationships when selecting a planet. It is no mistake that he sings these lines just before glancing at Nooshy and Klaus respectively at the beginning of the scene. Because the Sing movies are jukebox musicals, a lot of care needs to be taken when selecting the songs. However, this scene demonstrates that you can be creative with the execution of that song to achieve a more customised effect.

Secondly, Johnny's overall arc in the Sing series. In the first movie, he is the son of a gang boss, who expects him to join the 'family business'. But when Johnny chooses his dreams over his father (side note; Johnny causes the crash that prevents him from helping his father escape the cops, but not many people know that), Johnny's father disowns him, until he is forced to see his son's talent. He then proceeds to literally rip out the prison wall to support his son (in time to the music, I might add). In the second movie, Johnny's father supports his son's aspirations, even helping him fend off the hotel security trying to throw them out. While Johnny did show a level of aggression in the first movie when he's learning to be a getaway driver, this is the only scene where he's shown outright aggression as a means to an end, thereby becoming closer to his father. Now, this is just speculation, because there isn't much focus on one character in an ensemble movie, but I believe Johnny wouldn't have been as comfortable with aggression if he hadn't bonded with his father.

At each step of the way, *Illumination* carefully and skilfully crafted an entire story with a protagonist, antagonist, supporting characters, conflict, low point, and high point, with underlying themes to be gleaned, in a single scene. While I believe I have delved quite deep into this scene, I invite you to watch it for yourself and see if you can find anything I've missed. I also invite you to delve into a favourite scene of your own, whether you're a writer or not, just to gain a new appreciation of it as I have.

All in all, after just three and a half minutes, Johnny is no longer simply a theatre gorilla. He is a lover *and* a fighter.

(As a final note, and I would be remiss not to say it, Johnny's father's name is Big Daddy.)

worse

Milla Adams

They tell us not to be hungry, there are people who are starving.
They tell us not to be in pain, there are people in agony.
They tell us not to complain, there are people who have it worse.
They tell us 'Just push through', as if there's light on the other side.
They tell us our pain and woes are nothing, and maybe they are.
But they're not nothing to us, even though it could be worse.
They tell us not to crave pain, even though they're the ones who said,
That unless your pain is worse, you're not allowed to hurt.

Eaten From The Core

Xander Egan

The apple was said to be the fruit of knowledge.

It is a common myth that the hole in the apple came from a worm burrowing into the fruit. In reality, the female fruit fly lays her eggs inside of the apple flesh, allowing the worms to eat from the core and out to the skin. This is why you'll never find a hole from a worm burrowing its way in. A few bad apples won't ruin the rest of the worms mature into moths and flies though; although, all you'll see is the rind of a once good apple. Like an empty book cover.

The place I grew up in was a weird town. We were very secluded, and we were all obsessed with learning. Knowledge was the main thing we hungered for, like the worm with the apple. Everyone knew a lot, and we ordered a lot of books in from outside the walls. Well, they're not walls per se; our town was surrounded by tall mountains that only had one road in or out, and none of us owned a car. It'd be an annoyance to everyone in town to own a car because our roads were very thin. Everyone walked everywhere, and we enjoyed it.

I don't think I've properly introduced myself—my name is Arthur, and I'm a chemist who lives around the edge of the town. I work at a family-run chemist that everyone comes to. They can fill whatever prescriptions they may need filling, or if they just need some medicine quickly. I'm sure you know how a chemist works. I've been learning about chemistry all my life, almost as if it was my destiny. My father taught me everything he knew before he died, he was a good man. He encouraged me to be a pharmaceutical chemist.

So, I spent most of my days in the lab, making medicine for people. But every few weeks I had a day free, so I would make the trip to the centre of town, and catch up with some of my more scholarly friends. Each of them had their own thing, their shtick. For Jonathan it was physics, and Michael loved mathematics; but it was my childhood friend, Charlie—who double majored in psychology and religious studies—who seemed to be the most enthusiastic about his choice of study. Of course, we didn't understand it as well as he did, but he loved it more than we ever loved our studies. He would go on long-winded rants about how the human mind cannot begin to understand the truth behind religion and junk like that. To be fair, I never really paid attention. I was reading the books that I had bought.

I quite liked fiction, as well as my academic pursuits. I had a keen interest in fantasy, work set in the past, with science we can't use. I ate it up. My personal library was full of the classics, and a few lesser-known authors. I personally believe that we do have magic; it's just that we just understand it so well, that we call it chemistry. And if we did discover some sort of magic, how long until we would classify it under a new branch of science? That's just what I think anyway. And this story isn't about me. It's about my town, and how I had to watch it burn to the ground.

One day I went out into town, and was planning on meeting up with Jonathan, Micheal, and Charlie; but when I arrived at our usual hangout spot, no one was there. I looked around and I saw people making their way towards the park in the centre of our town. I followed them, spotting Charlie up on a makeshift stage, telling people about how he had a vision of God while he was sleeping. How he came down and told Charlie that everyone was living their lives wrong, and if they don't change themselves, they'll suffer eternally.

I didn't believe a word of it, but for some reason, everyone else ate it up. I watched as these people who were supposed to be men and women of science checked for something so unscientific; it made me feel sick to my stomach. I watched on for a few minutes, Charlie spewing this nonsense about how the truth of life was being delivered to his mind every night. The worst part to me was the fact that he looked like he *believed* this garbage. Eventually, I had enough of it and I marched my way through the crowd, pushing people away. I made it up to Charlie's makeshift stage and I grabbed him by his short golden hair and pulled him down into a huddle.

'Charlie, please tell me you don't actually believe this... this utter *nonsense*!' I pleaded, watching his expression shift from child-like glee to worry and confusion

'Arthur...You don't believe in the word of God?' he queried. I felt a sudden weight in my stomach. He actually believed what he was spewing. I stood back up and collected myself for a moment before I tried to get the people's attention.

'Attention, my fellow townsfolk! Why are all of you so quick to trust the words of a man whose claim we cannot prove? Are we not people of science, maths, and logic? We cannot simply trust this man because he is our friend; we must find a way to prove his claims of seeing and hearing this so-called 'God' before we jump to conclusions,' I exclaimed to the crowd. They sat silent for a moment, but then I heard a loud 'boo!' come out from one person. Then another. They all eventually began to slowly give up on their own morals and logic as they shunned me for only telling the truth. I felt a hand be placed upon my shoulder, and Charlie whispered into my ear.

'You might want to walk back home Arthur, and rethink what you've done. I'll give you a copy of our new religious text when I finish writing it, okay? Don't worry; there's still time to save yourself,' he told me, in a clearly fake helpful way. I swallowed my pride and began the walk back up to my house/lab.

The next month was slowly more and more concerning. First one person cancelled their prescription, then another, and another. Eventually, everyone in the town had cancelled their prescriptions. And it was after that happened that Charlie showed up at my door. Looking through the peephole, I could see that he was wearing an entirely red cloak and carrying a basket full of apples. I opened the door and asked him what on earth he was wearing.

'This is the garb that God has asked me to wear from now on. He also mandates that we must all eat an apple a day to make sure our knowledge can be retained properly, so I've brought you a few! Along with our new book full of God'steachings, we call it the Bible of Truths. Read up Arthur; I expect you to beat our next gathering in the town centre to discuss his further teachings!' he sped through while placing down the basket and pulling a book out of it before giving it to me and trying to turn away. I grabbed him by the shoulder and turned him back around.

'Look, we've been friends ever since your family moved to this town. I have been behind you on everything. But this is where I stop. You're being ridiculous. I am not going to be attending your gatherings. You may have brainwashed everyone else, seemingly without even trying. But you will not convert me.' I picked up the basket of apples and pushed it into his chest. 'Now, take your damn apples back, and leave me alone.'

We both just stood there for a few seconds. He looked down at his apples and then looked back at me with daggers in his eyes. He then turned and left, slamming the door behind him.

I was never one to turn down a book—I loved them. But something about the book he handed me felt off. Now, I'm no English major, but I was determined to analyse this book to see if there were any obvious flaws that I could use to pick apart his whole charade. I sat at my desk and took out an old notebook someone had given me years back. I'd considered it useless, but now it finally had a use. Guess everything has a use given enough time.

I began reading the book and writing down the main points it was making. Stuff like 'be kind unto others', 'eat an apple every day', 'pray before every activity you do', and some weird stuff. One of the 'lessons' was to not trust doctors, because they are secretly poisoning you. I even found some lessons that contradicted other lessons. One of them read 'If one cannot accept the true teachings, he must be considered an enemy and shamed until they realise their mistakes'—which felt like it went against the first lesson of being a kind person. I had made a decision to go to their next meeting and make my complaints known.

The next day, I woke up with a certain level of spite in my blood. I felt angrier than in previous days. I dressed and had an orange for breakfast before putting on my cloak and walking into the town centre. They had already set up chairs and a larger stage with an altar, along with a statue of Charlie. I audibly scoffed upon seeing this. It made me sick to my stomach that the people who I had once considered my friends had been turned to this false religion so easily.

I realised that I had gotten there a little earlier than I probably should have, so I walked to the nearby bookstore, looking for anything that could distract me from my rage. I walked inside and noticed that a lot of the shelves were empty. I felt a sense of unease, and wandered further through the shelves, looking to see if there was anything on the shelves. Eventually, I found a shelf, but it contained only one book on it. It had about a hundred copies of the new *Bibles of Truth*. I furrowed my brow and turned to leave. *What on earth had they done to my precious books*? I pondered as I made my way back to the town centre.

I waited for a while amongst the other townsfolk, and after what felt like ten eternities, the 'sermon' started. I sat and listened as Charlie spouted nonsense for half an hour, and then ended by telling them all, 'Give up everything that gives you pleasure and substitute it for pain. You need to know true pain and despair in order to be worthy of the eternal pleasure of heaven.'

I sat there, dumbfounded. No way he just told everyone that they had to give up all sources of happiness? I shot up from my seat and threw off the hood of my cloak, speaking up so that everyone who could hear me.

'People! Please don't give in to this nonsense! I have spent all of yesterday evening picking apart this so-called bible of 'truths' that this man has sold to all of you, and it is riddled with holes and contradictions! Think for yourselves like you used to do for a moment! If this God was real, wouldn't he show us all himself? Why would a truly loving deity conceal his form from everyone but one person? Please consider this before removing everything that makes you happy!'

This is all I could say before being tackled to the ground by police in red attire. I struggled and tried to get up, but I was quickly handcuffed, and I knew when I was beaten, so I gave up on resisting. I was pinned to the floor, and I could see Charlie's feet walking over to me. He snapped his fingers and the guards grabbed my hair from behind, pulling my head up to force me to look at Charlie again. He had covered the bottom half of his face with a mask painted with red paint, which made his lips look like he had just taken a bite of human flesh.

'Arthur...You goddamn disappointment. And to think I wanted you to join us,' he said before kicking me in the stomach. I fell to the floor again and curled up into the foetal position.

'Go. Search his house and confiscate anything that goes against our beliefs. We'll follow behind you,' he told the police, before kneeling down and yanking me to my feet. He whispered in my ear threatening me, 'Say another word and I won't hold back next time. Understood?'

I nodded, and we began walking up the hill toward my house.

Charlie had a death grip on my arm the whole way up. I didn't know what had gotten into him, but it was scaring me. We eventually reached my house and I was forced to unlock it and let the police search through all my belongings. They came out on multiple trips, taking out all of my chemistry equipment, my books—even my plates and utensils.

'You have one chance Arthur; you can willingly give this up, or we will have to burn it all. Nod yes to give up willingly; if no, then we will have to banish you from this town forevermore. Think long and hard and make your choice,' was the ultimatum that Charlie had offered me. I didn't know how to tell him that if he burned my stuff he would put everyone in danger; but even if I tried, he would hurt me, and not listen at all. I shook my head no, and spit in Charlie'sface. The police all drew their weapons, and pointed them at me. Charlie made them put their weapons down with a single gesture of his hand.

'He has made his choice; he is no longer part of this city, we have no jurisdiction over him.' He turned to me, unlocking my handcuffs. 'Now, Arthur. There is one road that goes in and out of this town. You know where it is. You will need to walk it until you find your next place of living. If I ever see your face in this town again. my guards will not be so kind. Now go.'

I couldn't believe he was just letting me go like that. I nodded, one last sign of the little respect that was still left for him, and I began running.

I ran for hours; all day, really. Only stopping at the occasional rock that was fit to sit on. Now and then there was a gap in the trees where I could see the town. As it got darker, the town looked brighter. Eventually, in the dead of midnight, I came to a clearing overlooking the town, and I saw the town I once called a home engulfed in flames. I stood for a moment, staring in horror. I was at such an elevation that I could see the entirety of my once great town. It was in the shape of an apple. Charlie was a worm that had been born inside of the apple, and now he had destroyed it from the core to the flesh.

I could hear him laughing.

carnival

keira cranley

The lights of the carnival shone over the harbour, reflected on the water like glittering stars splashed across the night sky. Zoe stood on the very edge of the foreshore, only a short distance away from the bustling carnival. The shouts and laughter of children echoed through the air, mixed in with the mechanical noise of show rides moving about, and the hollers of vendors calling out to potential customers. Zoe leaned back against a nearby fence, sighing softly. It had been nearly an hour since her friends were supposed to arrive. It was quite likely by now that they weren't coming. No, not likely. They simply weren't coming at all.

Zoe looked up briefly as the Ferris wheel stopped to let a group of teenagers on. That should have been her and her friends. Across from the Ferris wheel, a girl let out an excited squeal of delight, having won a giant teddy bear from some game. The girl jumped around, waving the oversized bear about.

Zoe turned away, to another section of the Carnival. Her eyes rested on a food vendor, presenting a deep-fried creation that vaguely resembled a giant spring roll to a customer. The customer turned around, showing the monstrosity to their friends who all ooed and ahhed. A pang of sadness hit her. She didn't want to believe her friends had abandoned her, but now that the last light of day was well and truly gone, Zoe knew that they had. She was alone, at a place people were meant to enjoy with their friends. Seriously, was *every* teenager in town here? She could see people from her high school and the neighbouring private school mingling in the crowd. There were even some out-of-towners around the place. And every last one of them looked like they were having the time of their life.

A few tears welled up in Zoe's eyes, blurring her vision. She wiped them away quickly, knowing that from where she stood, the carnival lights were shining directly on her face. She turned away from the lively carnival for a moment, trying to decide whether to stay by herself or just go home.

'Hello.'

Zoe jumped in surprise; she hadn't been expecting anyone else to be in this distant corner of the foreshore. She couldn't see anyone near her though and peered out into the darkness behind the carnie's mobile homes.

'Hello?' she called out into the gloom. No reply. Oh well. The person had probably been talking to someone else anyway. She turned away. A stick snapped behind her, in the direction she had just been looking. Zoe whipped her head around to see a figure stepping out of the darkness. It was a teenage boy, slightly taller than her, with long, blonde curly hair.

'Hey. I haven't seen your face around here before.' The boy stopped next to her, leaning against the fence. Now that he was illuminated by the carnival lights, she could see his features better. He had a gorgeous smile.

'I don't go out very often,' Zoe said shyly, averting her eyes from his strong gaze.

The boy nodded slowly before speaking again. 'So, what made you come out on this perfectly average night then? You here with friends?'

Zoe looked down. She didn't want to mention that she had been ditched by her friends and that she was all sad and lonely now. 'Um, I just wanted to get out of the house. Change of scenery, you know,' She said, trying to make it seem she was alone on the beach by choice.

The boy nodded again, his curls bouncing back and forth as he did. 'Nice, nice. I'm Alex, by the way.' He held out a hand. It took Zoe a moment to realise she was supposed to shake it.

'Zoe,' she said too quietly, before clearing her throat and repeating "Zoe" louder.

There was a brief silence, the cacophony of carnival noises becoming almost deafening for a moment before Alex spoke again. 'Well, I hope you don't mind me asking but might I keep you company for a while?'

Zoe smiled, nodding quickly. She was happy to have found a friend. *Or maybe something more*, she thought, noting the cheeky glint in Alex's eyes as he gently took her hand, leading her away from the dark fence line and into the colourful hubbub. He let go of her hand, walking backward as he talked with speed. It was clear he was the more extroverted of the pair, given the ease he was able to talk about anything and everything. Zoe didn't even listen to half of what he said, she was just happy to not be alone. How good it felt to have the night turned around completely.

'So, what do you think? You wanna go for it?' Alex asked, and Zoe snapped back to reality, realising she had no idea what he just asked.

'Uh sure, sounds great,' she answered quickly, having no clue what she was getting herself into. Alex just smiled and sped up his walk, ducking under a ride barrier. Zoe hesitated for a moment, trying to figure out where he was going.

'Come on!' he called out from up ahead. Zoe swallowed a lump in her throat and ducked under the barrier, running after him.

She was panting by the time she caught up with him. And then he was gone again. Zoe whirled around in confusion.

'Up here!' She looked up. He was hanging off the edge of the stationary carousel. Zoe's mouth fell open. How had he managed to get up there so fast? Alex cast a glance over his shoulder. 'Hurry!' he half whispered, half shouted.

Zoe looked past him and saw the source of his anxiety; the ride operator was about to start the ride. Not wasting another moment, Zoe dashed forward and grabbed the edge of the carousel, slipping about clumsily as she struggled to climb any higher. She could see people approaching, coming closer to take their seats on the fiberglass animals.

Suddenly, a pair of hands grabbed her and yanked her up onto the top of the carousel. Zoe gasped in fear as she almost slipped off again. Alex reached out to her and pulled her up to where she could grab a hold of the ornate central spire.

'There. I got you.' Zoe nodded shakily, squeezing her eyes tightly shut as the ride began. She held on tight, scared to slip right off the edge if she let go of the spire.

Alex chuckled when he saw Zoe's scrunched-up face. 'Hey, it's fine—this thing doesn't go very fast.' Zoe did not open her eyes; she was absolutely terrified. How had she let herself end up here, in this dangerous position way up high on top of a carousel? She should never have followed Alex.

'Zoe! It's okay, open your eyes.' Zoe shook her head timidly. She did not want to listen to him at all. 'Trust me Zoe, just open your eyes. I won't let you fall.' She felt him lift her into a more stable position atop the carousel.

'Trust me,' he whispered. She didn't want to at all, but curiosity got the better of her, and slowly, she opened her eyes.

'Wow,' was all she could say. She could see the entire carnival below her, from the colourful Ferris wheel at the entrance to the sideshow alley full of games and exhibits, all the way to the bumper cars whizzing around at speed. The whole area was brightly lit, shining gloriously in the night. It was so bright, she couldn't even see the usually starry night sky. Past the carnival and foreshore, she could see the faint outline of the sand dunes that ran along the whole length of the beach. And then as the carousel turned, she could see the distant city lights.

Alex looked out over the carnival grounds with her, the two of them watching the scenery as the carousel slowly turned around and round. He turned to her for a moment, 'It's amazing, isn't it?' Zoe nodded in agreement, mute with awe.

She felt herself becoming less scared as she held on to the central spire while the carousel continued to slowly turn. The carnivalgrounds all looked so small from up high. All the carnival-goers looked like tiny little ants skittering about from her vantage point. The spire rattled for a moment, and Zoe saw that Alex had climbed up right on top of the spire. He was very brave, she thought. She stayed where she was and soon Alex rejoined her. They locked eyes for a moment. Zoe was surprised she hadn't noticed the almost unreal shade of blue in his eyes earlier. She was dazzled, unable to look away. Alex began to make his way closer to her, smiling softly with a closed mouth.

The carousel came to a halt. Zoe and Alex both froze as the carousel shook slightly from riders hopping off. They waited a few minutes for more people to hop on, but no one did. Alex peeked over the edge. "They're shutting the ride for the night," he whispered to Zoe. She looked over the edge, seeing that some of the smaller rides were indeed starting to close. Her brow furrowed. How late was it? Maybe Alex had a watch.

'Alex,' she said, nudging his shoulder with her elbow. The only acknowledgment of the gesture came in the form of an agitated 'Shush'. Alex was still looking over the edge.

Zoe followed his gaze. The carousel operator was just about to leave for the night. But he lingered at the edge of the carousel for a long moment.

'Hey!' the operator shouted, looking up and pointing directly at Alex and Zoe. They had been spotted. Alex jumped up, balancing perfectly as he quickly made his way to the edge of the carousel's curved roof.

'*Hey!*' the operator shouted again, louder this time. He was attracting the attention of the other carnival-goers now. People began looking up at the top of the carousel, worry and fear showing on their faces.

'Zoe! Come on!' Alex called, having made his way to the very edge. But Zoe hung on tight, too scared to let go. She was lying on an angle, her feet facing the edge. If she let go and slipped, she would fall straight down.

'Are you crazy? Get down from there!' The angry shout of the operator caused her to let go in a panic. She slid straight down the curved surface, falling right off the edge. Zoe screamed as she fell. And then she wasn't falling anymore. She had landed hard on the ground below. Pain shot up her side. All the air had been knocked right out of her. She was yanked to her feet before she even had time to fully process what happened. Alex threw his arm around her and pulled her away from where she had fallen. The operator had called security, who were now running after them at full speed. Alex dragged Zoe into a narrow alcove.

'You hurt?' he asked. Zoe shook her head. The pain had gone now. She was pretty sure she was just shocked. Suddenly, a light shone into the alcove. Security. Alex grabbed Zoe's hand and pulled her out of the alcove. They ran with speed down Sideshow Alley, past the Ferris wheel, and jumped into the closed bumper car arena. Zoe and Alex dodged the stationary cars, climbing the back fence and falling into the caravan park. Alex took off immediately as soon as he hit the ground, but Zoe looked back for a moment. Security didn't seem to know where they were. Zoe breathed a sigh of relief. And then a bright torchlight shone directly onto her face, blinding her. Clumsily, Zoe scrambled to her feet and ran after Alex.

'Zoe!' She ran after the sound of his voice.

'Alex!'

'Over here!' Zoe kept running. Without the carnival lights, the night was pitch black. Zoe fell several times, sand and mud covering her clothes. She couldn't tell where she was.

And then a pair of arms circled around her. Zoe gasped, thinking she had been caught. 'Zoe! It's me!'

She turned and hugged Alex tightly. After a moment, she stepped back. 'Whew. I didn't think we'd get away. I haven't run that fast in ages,' Zoe said, panting between words. Her eyes slowly adjusted to the darkness around her. 'Are we in... a cave?' she asked, reaching a hand out to touch the nearest wall. It was smooth and rocky.

Alex nodded. 'Yeah.'

Zoe turned away from the wall, back to Alex. 'Thanks. For everything.' She blurted out. 'I had fun at the carnival, even though it was scary.' She hesitated a moment before going on. 'I was actually meant to meet some friends tonight, but they never showed up, so I just wanted to say I really appreciate you saying hello to me.' Zoe could faintly see the outline of Alex's face in the dark.

'Your friends ditched you?' he asked. Zoe couldn't tell if he sounded sincere or thoughtful. 'Well, they clearly wouldn't miss you if anything happened to you.' A pang of fear shot through her heart with these words. She felt him lean in close. She stepped back, a rush of butterflies fluttering through her stomach. She looked around desperately. How had she gotten into the cave? She couldn't see the exit anywhere.

Alex grabbed her chin suddenly, forcing her to look at him. Zoe gasped as Alex smiled wildly, baring all of his teeth. There was something wrong with some of them. They were unusually sharp, glinting in the soft moonlight that was shining through a hole in the top of the cave.

'What are you doing?' Zoe stammered. Her heart began to race. She was confused as to why Alex's demeanour had changed so suddenly. Zoe tried to push him away, but he was too strong.

'It's a pity you're so trusting.'

In one quick motion, he sunk his teeth into her neck. Zoe screamed and kicked out wildly but to no avail. He wasn't letting go.

'Please, stop!' she begged, grabbing at his face. He pushed her away with force, sending her flying into the wall. She landed with a sickening thud; the world spun around her, everything going blurry. She felt blood drip down from her head and throat, fat rivulets. She held a hand to her neck, screaming when she felt a chunk of skin missing.

Alex knelt in front of her. Zoe pushed herself as far back into the wall as she could go, like a cornered animal. He reached out, gently cupping her face in his hand. Zoe shuddered and tried to slap him away but missed. She was seeing double.

'I would apologise for this, but I'm just so hungry.' Alex smiled sickeningly, baring his grotesque teeth at her again. Zoe looked away, tears streaming down her face.

'Ah, why am I saying anything? You'll be dead soon anyway.' Alex laughed before biting down on Zoe's neck again. She could feel the blood being drained from her, could feel the life leaving her body as she drifted slowly into darkness.

I SUPPOSE THIS IS IT

Jenna Lockley

I suppose this is it.

I am standing in front of the branching path; both metaphorically, and the multiverse power of the same name.

The bar is moderated by the O.P.C.: The Omniverse Preservation Cooperative. Maybe they'll see I mean no harm. It'd be nice not to be at gunpoint for once, but considering what they thought I was. . .

I sigh, remembering waking up for the first time.

My first thought hadn't truly been my own. It was the machine that I'd grown in. It was listing facts about me, so my creators didn't have to; basic things like 'you eat energy', and 'you can disguise yourself as other creatures', and 'you don't need to breathe'.

Then things began to break down. 'You are *error* based life form', and '*error* are a lie', it told me.

Once it was done, I left that abandoned place quickly; the multiverse called.

Magic. Science. Horror. Chivalry. Madness. *Family*. I discovered these, and so much more! But my appetite served as a problem. It didn't start out bad; a light bulb here, a wand there, and I was good to go. Slowly though, it grew stronger. That's when trouble started to follow me. In the meantime, I made friends, enemies, and the like. Only one of each could follow me through the worlds, though.

The friend I made is a mage named Jocea, a half-dragon born to a world of spacefaring gods. Whereas my enemy is an Organisation, so my previous statement was misleading—but they all work under the same banner:

The O.P.C.

I don't know how they find and follow me, but I do know how they heard of me. I had been helping a superhero that I knew, Intercontinental Ballistic Lance, with a villain that could shoot orbs of fire out of a cursed fire extinguisher, the Fire Distinguisher™. They had been chucking fire left and right. Just looking at it had made me hungry. So I took the Fire Distinguisher—the item, not the person—and ate it. In my defence, it was very effective. But I had forgotten that that world was in what I call an 'Internet Age', so the video of me eating it went 'infectious' on 'us roll'; and from that point on, they were after me.

It took a long time for me to figure out *why* they didn't like me. It hadn't occurred to me that eating energy was a problem, except for possibly quickening the heat death of that particular universe. I suppose I was doing that, but that isn't why it was a problem. I got ambushed several times before I realised they were serious. From there, I began to research them. There was no date of creation for the O.P.C. because they'd decided to build their base outside of time and space—to be showy, I guess. But from there, their goal was unwavering.

To protect the Multiverse.

This was something I could respect; they make sure that gods, corporations, and the like don't go and take over everything. It was their *methods* that spooked me. Spying, brainwashing, and erasing were all things they were willing to do to keep their version of peace. That, and their world-spanning presence made them the Illuminati, but with extra steps. So I assumed, incorrectly, that they wanted me gone because of my powers. That, or this was their version of hiring someone. Either way, I wasn't interested.

At this point, my hunger had grown. The one light bulb had become one generator, but it wasn't concerning me yet, so I continued with life. I hung out with Jocea, and I researched.

The O.P.C. was a side project. My true desire was my *purpose*. The tube that I'd awoken in was old and broken, and the area around it wasn't doing much better. Since I'd left almost immediately, I didn't know much about my origin, other than what had been spared from the static.

But I do know one thing; you don't make a shapeshifting energy using a blob for no reason. Even if I was a prototype, even if I was a failure, at least I would know.

The biggest problem that I had was my memory. I wouldn't describe it as bad, but I wouldn't describe it as good. So, my time was dedicated to triangulating my home world's position. Or squareangulating, orconeangulating, or parallelogramangulating, depending on which of my friends you asked.

Once my friends began to notice my hunger too, I admit that I got scared.

The idea of them learning the truth scared me so much I'd avoid the question. I'd pretend not to hear, make excuses to leave—average things one does with question-avoiding. But being friends with detectives, magic users, and abstract concepts, means secrets aren't easy to keep. Meanwhile, the O.P.C. kept looking for me. I had the sense to tell my friends about them, at least. I had a friend who was a manifestation of the concept of security to help me with the firewalls to the database of the O.P.C. They'd suggested that the O.P.C. may know where I came from, given they were after me. This was the first time I heard of the idea that someone knew more about my history than me, despite my efforts. I did not heed that idea until much later, but admitted it was interesting.

Interesting is what I'd called it, but I could think of so many other ways to describe it now. Horrifying and devastating come to mind.

Regardless, we continued. Around this time, the O.P.C. had increased the amount of times they ambushed me. They were changing their plans. But since I could jump worlds, there wasn't much they could do. It was very annoying, but I began to notice that they *really* wanted to bring me in for some reason. The hunger was noticeably worse at this point. I had to eat exponentially more to stay full. By now I could no longer hide it from my friends, and I had to tell them of my appetite.

While most still welcomed me with open arms, Intercontinental Ballistic Lance was forced to kick me out of their city. The risk of me eating the crystals that gave the heroes their powers was too great. I understood the decision was not made by Lance, but rather by the city council. But man, it stung.

With more determination than ever, I pressed on. Researching, regular searching, and so on. If I stopped working, I'd think about how hungry I was. It was either study, or run from the O.P.C., which had gotten desperate, but not necessarily better—given they didn't have any tools that could actually grab a world-jumping, living liquid. I'm not sure if my friends worried about me, as I didn't check on them. I was too worried about my condition and what it would lead me to do. I was getting as desperate as the O.P.C. was. I kept searching and kept getting worse until finally, I found something.

It was a heavily redacted file buried deep within the reopened cases box. It described a facility that created semi-organic weapons. It was my best shot. This discovery and my growing hunger led me to write a letter to my friends. I told them of the state of my appetite, my discovery, and that I would not return until I was safe to be around again, thanking them for all they had done for me. The only person who could seek me out after this was Jocea, but she was dealing with an evil twin brother that she never knew she had, so I didn't think she'd show. Looking back makes me realise I *may* not be that smart.

I arrived at the place where the O.P.C. had fought someone. It was a cold broken place. The date hadn't been redacted, but anything related to time was corrupted from outside sources. It was because the world had so many holes at its physics and time. There were places with failed gravity, rocks falling eternally in a time loop, and once I entered the building, power to random machines were still on as energy refused to disperse into heat and light.

I was elated. Not by the state of the world, but this madness and disorder was a part of my first memories. I'd found it, my birthplace. Made place? Whatever. Due to the destruction of linear time, everything looked just as I remembered. I even found the pod that I came out of. It was just as broken and buried under rubble as before. I had to move on, but I did find what my 'name' was. D.J/S.D.P _45. I didn't know what that meant, but luckily that secret didn't take long to discover.

Not too far away from my pod was what appeared to be a lab. The outside computers, like most other things, had been stolen or smashed by rubble. However, the data storage itself looked untouched; it had been saved by being hidden by a now-decayed painting. The door had been rusted shut by time, so I had to teleport past it. Like everything else, the data storage was old. But it wasn't entirely destroyed or gone. I was overjoyed that my luck had finally turned around. I wouldn't use that word now, but I needed to see what was in there.

The names of those who made me both the company of the scientists will never be known, they had been erased from existence entirely. But what I was and what was made for was as clear as day. Was as the file described it a Dimension Jumper Subdivision Possessor Number Forty-Five. I was designed to jump into a universe with powerful people, choose the most powerful, hollow out the body, eat the soul and power inside, and then turn the skin into a flesh suit—taking their place as a puppet for my creators. Giving up my powers, for those my victim had. In hindsight, I may have given the O.P.C. too much flack with the Illuminati comparison, when I seem to be a slightly more complex version of 'The Thing'.

There weren't just possessors either; there were soldiers who had immense strength instead of shape-shifting and hollowing out, a winged division that could fly and be air support—even a clairvoyant division that was under development before everything went wrong. I wasn't just made as a weapon—I was made as a part of an army. I now understood why the O.P.C. believed I was a threat. I delved deeper into the files, looking for my biology, when the weight of everything hit me.

My hunger wasn't abnormality, it was by design. The appetite for energy had been shared by the whole army, starting when we first started eating. For me, that was supposed to be possession; the growth of this unending hunger was to keep us from defecting, as my creators were the only ones who could reset it to its initial state. I quickly looked into how they stopped it; I found some form of stasis pod that could reset the hunger. But looking at the map, I knew they weren't they weren't there anymore. Because they were in the lab that I'd just passed, the same one that was now essentially empty. I panicked for a second; the world wasn't broken enough for that much matter to disappear.

The way the area had been wrecked suggested that it had been stripped of anything deemed useful by the perpetrators, which explained why they couldn't get to the database that was hidden; or the device holding me that was under rubble. But who would take any of this stuff? The only people who would need it would be people who already knew about it—

Oh.

The O.P.C. knew. On reflection, they knew all of it. That's why they kept sending people after me. They knew I was a ticking time bomb of hunger. They must've tried to catch me via the plans my creators made, but because I never took someone's place it didn't work, so they had to improvise. If they had those computers, then maybe they had the pods too.

I heard a pile of metal clunk in the background behind me. Instinctively, I turned to look. Turned out Jocea had followed me to this place to confront me about it after I had sent the letter to her. I told her my discoveries here and that I was going to the O.P.C., as they seemed to be my only option, due to the blueprints for the pods being corrupted. She... did not like that. We had a small argument, but it was cut short. The evil twin brother that Jocea had, Malice, had followed Jocea to ambush her for reasons that he rambled so long and evilly about, that I stopped paying attention. But they started to fight, and I got caught up in it when Malice grabbed me. He had stabbed me in the face and on instinct, I had tried to absorb it. I did... but too well.

Once I opened my eyes, I realised what I had done. The dagger was in pieces, but so was every bone in Malice's arm. He was on the ground, his breaths laboured and shallow. I turned to see Jocea staring at me in horror and disbelief. She looked at Malice, then back at me, she opened her mouth to speak and I warped before she could say a word.

The world I crashed into was storming; very considerate of the world to be thematic for what I was emotionally going through.

I had almost killed Malice. I didn't know how Jocea would react, and I was too much of a coward to find out. On one hand, Malice was mad and more than willing to kill for his goals. On the other, Jocea didn't care about that; she couldn't stand the idea that her brother wasn't beyond redemption. But would she feel the same for me now that I'd done this? What I did was an accident, she knew of my hunger. But what was the point in apologising if I couldn't promise this wasn't going to happen again? The question wasn't whether or not I could face her after what I did, but whether it would matter. After thinking over my options, I'd decided I was too dangerous.

So here I am now in front of the branching path.

I either turn away and try to find my way out of this, or I enter the bar and hand myself over to the people who have been hunting me down. I can't say I'm not terrified; I've procrastinated by reliving my life's story. But as far as I can see I have no other option.

I go in.

The bar is what is expected of a multiverse inclusive area; a place so wildly varied it is one of the few places I don't stand out. I sit at the bar, looking at the menu, wondering what the normal procedure for giving yourself up to the law in a bar is.

If only there was an option on the menu for that. I turn the menu over to see that there is indeed a self-surrender special. *Huh, well I'll be.*

A bartender comes to check on me. 'Hey, why the short face?' He laughs at his joke, as he is a psychic horse. I don't want to draw too much attention to myself, so I point at the self-surrender option on the menu.

'Ah, hayseeds, I can't read... I'll get someone else, hold on.' He stands there for a bit, psychically calling someone else. But as the other person approaches, we lock eyes, and I realise this is the Captain that the O.P.C. had assigned to hunt me down. They flip an alarm, causing metal sheets to cover the doors and windows.

'*Why are you here*?!' She yells.

'*To turn myself in*!' I say.

'*What?!*'

Typical, I try to do something for the O.P.C., and they raise the alarm so they can't hear me.

Rufus turns off the alarm.

'*I'm here to*—I'm here to turn myself in.'

'*False alarm, everyone!!*' Rufus calls out.

Everyone comes out from hiding, some grumbling about filing a complaint, as Rufus uses telekinesis to slap the back of the Captain's head with a magazine.

'Sorry; Captain here meant no harm.' I don't believe him—I knew customer service mode when I heard it. But I play along.

'You're really doing this?' Captain asks, seeming unsure. I nod, explaining what had happened on my home world.

Rufus nods in sympathy, and Captain seems surprised that I only just found my origin, and wrote it down. She asks, 'Do you want a normal or deluxe cell?'

That intrigues me. 'What's the difference?' I ask.

'Deluxe costs thirty currency.'

Oh, for void's sake! 'I'll take normal, I still have *some* dignity.'

'Alright, follow me, Rufus says.

I follow him as he trots into a hallway behind the bar. We arrive at two doors. One says Cell and the other says the same thing, but has a star sticker on it. The door without a sticker opens. The room has one bed and four walls, but I didn't expect any more than that.

He left. I feel the weight of my decision come to fill the void. It wasn't the crushing, anxiety-inducing feeling from before I made the decision. It was more melancholy and heavy, more final. I don't know what's going to happen next. I don't know if it's going to turn out okay. But I know where to go from here and I know my end goal. For now, I've done all I can; I shall wait for the future to come to me and greet it as I always have.

Hyperfocus

Alistair Howie

Once upon a time, there was a company called the Happiness, Equity, and Love Company.

One of the workers here is named Herrsvanika.

Herrsvanika sighs:

What a bore.

She is in the lunchroom, sitting alone.

She looks at the clock.

She talks to herself:

When will this nightmare end?

Herrsvanika looks at her watch.

The clock chimes.

One of Herrsvanika's co-workers approaches her and asks:

Herrsvanika, why don't you come over and talk about your achievements; everyone is interested in what you have to say!

Herrsvanika replies:

Ehehe, I'm not much of a people person, as you can see.

Herrsvanika points high at the top of the room to the employee of the month sign. It says ninety-nine months.

As you can see I have no life except work, as it's one of the most enjoyable aspects of my life.

Herrsvanika's co-worker:

Herrsvanika, you need to take a break, as you have been putting a massive strain on your mental health. Also, the reason you enjoy work so much is that you don't want to move out of your comfort room!

Herrsvanika is fuming and pouting as she is being given criticism. She replies in a way that is defensive and aggressive:

Well, *it's because none of this interests me, as you can clearly see. Do you think I enjoy being surrounded by all these idiots, with their incessant obsession with small talk? That is why I love to isolate myself. And because of that, the results show that it's fine and I don't have* mental health issues.

The co-worker understands and leaves to join the other members of the team.

Another member of the team asked the member who was talking to Herrsvanika:

So, how did it go asking Heresy Wersey to join?

Co-worker one:

It went as well as you would expect— she got mad.

Co-worker two:

Maybe we could get Alastair to convince her to take a break.

Co-worker one:

Well, Alastair is away with his children, so we will have to wait till he gets back to make our move. However, we could work out Herrsvanika's schedule and sabotage her to make it look like she is suffering from bad luck; that will happen due to her not taking care of herself.

Co-worker three:

I feel like that will not work. As you know, Herrsvanika is a cautious individual, so she will most likely see any of your attempts coming from a mile away.

Co-worker one:

Yes, how could I forget? If we are going to do something like this then, we will have to make it multi-staged to keep Herrsvanika guessing!

While the co-workers are scheming, Herrsvanika is going to her office. She is sitting down and looking at a photo of her and her two younger sisters. She smiles.

An audible knock is heard on the outside of the door accompanied by some distant footsteps. Herrsvanika gets up. She places the photo frame on her desk, then goes over to the door and walks out of her room.

Co-worker one quickly walks into the room. They look around, trying to think of what to do. The co-worker has an idea. They put water on Herrsvanika's seat and walk out of the room.

Herrsvanika walks back into her room and scratches her head.

Well, that was strange. I guess I better go back to work.

Herrsvanika goes to sit down.

Do they really think they can get me that easily?

Herrsvanika picks her chair up and throws it out her door. She walks out of her office, stepping over the chair, and yells:

Who had the sheer audacity to place water on my chair?

The co-workers are watching from the background.

Well, that didn't work. Next plan?

The co-workers are sitting at a circular table.

Co-worker one:

So, what is our plan of attack? As the water on the seat didn't work. Herrsvanika has a white chair, so she saw the water puddle. . .

Co-worker two:

A whoopee cushion could work? Herrsvanika won't expect it at all because she will be too focused on her work!

Co-worker three:

That is a terrible idea; a whoopee cushion is pink and her seat is white. She will see it coming and will throw it into the main area again, and scream about people sabotaging her work!

Co-worker one:

What about a bucket of water on top of the door in her office? She'll get soaking wet!

Co-worker two:

No, what about a fish?
Co-worker three:
What, these won't work at all!

Meanwhile...

Herrsvanika walks around the office; she gets out a glass of water. Herrsvanika drinks the water. She then puts the water glass on the bench and walks back to her office.

She sees that the door is halfway closed. She nudges the door and the bucket falls, and the water goes everywhere. She goes to her chair and sees the whoopee cushion. She throws it out the door when all of a sudden the co-workers run past Herrsvanika to her office and throw a fish at her face before running away.

She falls to the ground. She grabs at the fish; Herrsvanika then runs after her coworkers.

She screeches:

Someone's getting fished tonight.

The co-workers are running around the building, and see on the noticeboard that Alastair is coming back from his vacation in 24 hours.

Herrsvanikais on a wheelie chair with her fish in hand.

In her head:

I must get 100 months of Employee of the Month as it is the only way I can achieve true happiness.

Voice is heard.

I'm back.

Alastair has returned to the building.

The co-workers run past Alastair.

Alastair's head turns to see where they're running to.

Herrsvanika screams:

Alastair, move out of the way!

Suddenly, a massive crash happens in the middle of the entrance of the building.

A crowd of co-workers gather to see what happened.

They see that Herrsvanika has crashed into Alastair.

Herrsvanika gets up and is horrified that she crashed into her boss.

She checks to see if he is okay.

He gets up.

Herrsvanika asks:

Are you okay, Alastair; do you need any help?

Alastair puts his hand on Herrsvanika's head and rubs it.

I'm fine, what about you?

Herrsvanika turns around and starts cursing at her co-workers for being big bullies.

These bozos have been harassing me because they are jealous of the fact that I've been the employee of the month for ninety-nine months straight. Could you tell them to leave me alone?

Alastair:

Herrsvanika, the reason they have been doing that is because they want you to take a break; they care for your well-being.

Herrsvanika proclaims:

I know that, but the 100-month streak needs to be completed, as I made my intention clear from the start.

Alastair:

Ah yes, how could I forget? That is why I would like to present this.

Alastair pulls out a box of chocolates.

Here you go!

Herrsvanika looks down at the chocolates.

She picks one and places it in her mouth

Nomnom nom; Herrsvanika's mouth cringes.

She spits it out and sticks her tongue out.

Rum and raisin ewwww!

She proceeds to throw the chocolates at the wall.

Alastair pulls out the 100-month plaque. This causes Herrsvanika's eyes to light up.

Alastair then back peddles to the door. Herrsvanika follows suit.

Alastair places the 100-month plaque down on the ground.

Herrsvanika picks up the plaque and hugs it.

Alastair then walks back to the door and closes it gently.

A faint word comes from Alastair's mouth.

Congratulations, Herrsvanika! Now be free!

THE SMOKER'S CAGE

JASMINE PUNGER-GLASS

The floor is painted cement
Grey, whether with paint or
The stain of innumerable ashes
One cannot truly discern

Benches line the perimeter
Uncomfortable at best
Suffer stains from many a coffee mug
Brown, watery ringworms

Metal and glass encase the space
Sad souls and laughter alike
Creating a micro-ecosystem
Which only those partaking can stand

At times a hazy fog appears
Built by tendrils of smoke

Curling upward gently
To join hands with their like
Ash flicks willy-nilly
Building swirling ashy dunes
That move as subtly as sand
Collecting here, now there

Legs bounce and splay
Spreading hues of grey waste
Hands gesticulate with animation
Sometimes as an attempt of normalcy

Eyes dance and squint
Between rising smoke
Mouths pursed around a filter
Now a hole that spills white clouds

Many seek solace in this wasteland
Hoping for a reprieve from pain
Others seek a lighter pleasure
That come with companionable understanding

THE INSURRECTIONISTS

JESSE KYAMBADDE

'Grit is the antithesis of Stubbornness. Where stubbornness is for a person to grudge and hold onto their faults, Grit is to persist on your mission and remove your flaws.'

Jesse Kyambadde, 2023

A superpower virus has impacted the world. An airborne virus with no symptoms, with a very small chance of creating an unforeseeably randomised superpower. Superhuman individuals have grouped together to protect their families against this harsh new Earth. World superpowers have also recruited armies of Heroes into an organisation named The League, who hunt, imprison, and destroy rogue superhumans with dangerous powers.

Another small group has formed out of some superhumans who try to defend themselves and their loved ones from other forces. This small group is called: The Insurrectionists.

-Part 1-

A wasteland of earthy tones is all that is left of this part of the city.

Raids, attacks, and a government organization called The League have destroyed the infrastructure of the city, letting the buildings disintegrate. Within the rubble a figure moves. A human. A *superhuman*. Someone brave enough to leave their home and venture out into the wasteland. The figure has a team assembled, ready to fight for their lives. The figure stands upon the rubble and comically falls over onto the rubble. A cloud of dust flies up around them, and their teammates scold them.

"Come on buddy, we have a mission."

The figure stands up and dusts their clothes. Their name is Sam, but all their friends and enemies call them by another name: Grit.

Maybe Grit was named this because they were insignificant in the team; maybe because of their sometimes-misplaced fearlessness. The other figures emerge. Thomas and Erica are their names, although they are not referred to by these.

Grit follows their comrades to a strange location: Metal plating surrounds the entrance to an imposing structure. A tower built by one of the most funded operations on the planet. The League. As Grit and the others get to the tower, they contemplate their decisions.

After surveying the building, Grit asks, 'Can you blast your way inside that thing?'

Thomas replies without hesitation. 'It's made of tungsten, remember? Extremely tough metal I can't melt. So, no, I can't.'

Erica sighs and furrows her brow, glancing at Grit. Now the team would have to find another way in. Thomas makes a snarky remark to Erica. 'Can you scream your way in for us?'

'No... maybe? Want me to try?' She replies. They shook their heads. Nobody wanted a superpowered blast to the ears today. Their only option for entry is Grit. It is their time to shine.

'I can be bait,' offers Grit.

With no options left, the others try to force their way into the tower. Thomas attempts to use a combustive blast to melt the metal, and Erica tries a sonic scream to reverberate the door open. Grit sat against the tower and deeply exhales. They felt like their power wasn't applicable, but it still put a target on their back. On all their backs.

Erica stands at the door. No damage. She tries to search for any exploitable weakness. Highly secured: ID, Voice control, reinforced. 'Huh, voice control.'

Grit could see, based on her face, that Erica guessed it wasn't so secure after all. By channelling her vocal manipulation abilities into the lock, she could mess with the software. They all knew it. After mimicking a few voices she had heard from previous encounters with League members, the door opened.

'That's why they call me Mockingbird,' she spoke softly. 'Get in here; we need to stop this Bug character.'

'Yeah, when we destroy that guy, The League might leave us alone,' Thomas replies.

'What if the tower has a self-destruct or something?' asks an anxious Grit.

Thomas gave them a short answer. 'We already have an explosive-capable guy here. I'll just blow them up first.'

As the Insurrectionists advanced through the tower, they stumble across a few armed League members; none of which were superpowered. One of them shouts: '*What are you doing in here?*'

Thomas saw his chance to step up. As the League members readied their weapons, he smiles. A great flash and wave of heat tears through the air, smoke flooding the room. Thomas steps out of the explosion's radius, unharmed.

Mockingbird claps her hands. 'Can't believe you named yourself after a cannon: it doesn't even have a brain.'

Thomas, aka Cannoneer, replies hastily, 'And I can't believe you named yourself after a bird... brain.'

Grit had heard these petty insults before. Most of the Insurrectionists had spent their lives in hiding, and not getting a good education.

Alarms began blaring.

'Great— now we're going to get swarmed by the League,' sighs Cannoneer.

A figure steps out from the still apparent smoke, the haze shrouding their silhouette. It was their target: The Bug. As The Bug emerges, she slowly claps her hands.

'Well done. You found me.' She says sarcastically. As The Bug closed the space between them, Grit and their accomplices felt their minds numbing. The Bug's power was working.

Mockingbird let out a gasp as she tried resisting, struggling to speak. 'You won't search our minds this easy... My friends are a. . . blank slate.'

The Bug stood above the group as they lost feeling, their minds becoming open to Psychic interference. Grit was resisting well, but their powers of Adaption required time to become strong. They couldn't adapt to the interference in time to stop it. As a last-ditch attempt, Cannoneer fires a combustive shot into the room. Unfortunately, The Bug was able to sense them thinking about it, and dove out of the way, as best they could.

Boom! Everything was silent, the mental fuzz dissipating. As the Insurrectionists regain focus, they see The Bug has been engulfed by the blast and knocked unconscious.

'Couldn't predict that one, could you?' Cannoneer jeers. Grit and the Insurrectionists got to work looting the building.

'Found some records of us here,' exclaims Grit, tearing up papers.

'When we are done, we'll blow this stuff up right?' Asks Grit, unsettled by the detailed reports.

And so, they destroyed the documents. And it should've been easy.

Should've.

-Part 2-

Our protagonists return to the place they call home. Abound in rubble and broken-down vehicles, the entrance was shrouded by drapes of cloth, used to conceal it. Grit, Mockingbird, and Cannoneer enter the hideout. Grit splits off from their mission buddies to find their friend Gabbro. Gabbro was a mentor for Grit, as they had the same powers. Grit knew that Gabbro had endured a lot.

Gabbro saw Grit, and their face lit up. Grit sat opposite them on a rusty chair, kicking their legs up on the weathered table.

Gabbro eyes Grit. 'How'd the mission go? You destroy the documents?'

'Yep, we got Bug too. Cannoneer locked them up or something.'

Gabbro was a pacifist, and was averse to violence, but understood how vile Bug was. Gabbro nods, relief evident on their face.

'I remember fighting off the League. They're too strong. Best to escape and evade,' Gabbro says softly.

Grit had heard this before. They say in return, 'What kind of powers have you got to help you escape and evade?'

Gabbro let out a sigh. The core message of their teachings often went ignored.

'I've got some resistance to heat, some speed. I can climb well.'

Grit felt heavier, Disappointment filling them. The best person they knew at using their power of adaptation had nothing but basic parkour to offer. Grit had hoped that they could get some cool new powers from fighting Bug. Maybe telekinesis, or mental resistance at least. But they had developed nothing. Maybe they would have fewer headaches in the future, that's all. Powers that seemed futile to them.

A forlorn frown developed on Grit's face. Having spent so much time together, Grit knew that Gabbro could tell Grit was feeling sad. Although Gabbro didn't understand Grit's past struggles, they could relate to the hurt of being hunted by The League.

'Anything bothering you?'

Grit could never understand the inequity of superpowers. Why some people got some, others didn't. Even though Grit had powers, they were useless. And worst of all, they were still in danger of The League, because their ability was 'potentially dangerous'. Grit wouldn't join The League because the entire organisation was built on killing others. And the security for superhumans who joined would be threatened, once dangerous hits were no longer a problem. The League hunt themselves, then?

This was all a lot for Grit. A lot was bothering them. But they didn't answer; Grit merely shook their head.

'Nope, just still disoriented.'

Grit got up to leave. Gabbro had seen them like this before, but they knew that their advice wouldn't stick. Maybe Grit has to learn from experience, instead.

Maybe Grit has to learn from experience...

As Grit began to leave, Gabbro got up to follow them, calling out to get Grit's attention. Excitement tinging their words, Gabbro came up with a plan.

'How about we go scale a wall? I can show you my sub-par wall crawling. You might learn something.'

Grit's eyes lit up. They would do something.

'Let's go.'

The two exit the hidden sanctuary to explore the wilderness, hopefilling them. They would navigate old decaying buildings full of new experiences to learn from.

-Part 3-

Gabbro and Grit walk across the concrete gravel and rusty pipelines of the abandoned city. The crunch of stones underfoot made less sound than the cry of creaking metal in the distance. In this lonely silence, feelings of discomfort were amplified. To lighten the mood, Gabbro says jokingly, 'You know, if you pretend that the creaking metal is a bunch of happy cows in a field, it feels a lot nicer walking here.'

Grit smiles half-heartedly. 'I guess so.'

As the two walk, they took in their surroundings. It wasn't much, but after the Virus had afflicted the world and brought dangerous superpowers, anything that kept you safe from The League was home. After some minutes of walking, they got to an intact wall with holds on it.

Gabbro turns to Grit. 'I want you to be prepared to escape The League if worst comes to worst. And climbing walls is something they can't do with their heavy armour.'

Grit nods in understanding as Gabbro demonstrates. They put themselves against the wall, scaling it slowly using the footholds. Grit was underwhelmed.

'Is that superpowered or just normal?' Asks a forlorn Grit.

Gabbro replies with a chuckle. 'Normal, just so you can see what I'm trying to do here. I can climb a lot faster than this.'

To Grit, this was such a lame excuse for a deadly power. Climbing faster, of all things, had put both of them on the League's hit list. Grit let out a yawn and sat down on some old pavement.

Gabbro was halfway down the wall when they froze; they were glancing around at the broken-down cars and scorched roads. They seem to have spotted something, and Grit could tell something was wrong. Gabbro slowly descends the wall and makes it back to Grit.

'We have to move. Be very quiet,' Whispers Gabbro.

Grit trusted Gabbro's word, following them. They walk hunched over behind as much cover as possible to avoid the entity that Gabbro had spotted nearby. Every few seconds Gabbro looks over their shoulder to check if anything is there, Grit walking behind Gabbro. A crunch was heard. Gabbro stops in their tracks and slowly tugs them to the floor.

'What was that?' Grit whispers.

'League member,' quietly replies to Gabbro. 'I shouldn't have taken you out here.'

All at once, many crunches were heard, surrounding the two. A gruff voice shouts, voice ringing in the debris of concrete, 'We have you surrounded! Immediately show yourself!'

Gabbro slowly stands up, Grit doing the same. They could see the League members surrounding them with weapons, about ten soldiers, most likely a scouting unit. The same soldier shouts to the pair, 'Put away your hands and prepare for apprehension! Resistance will be met with severe force!'

Soldiers began to close in to handcuff Gabbro and Grit. Gabbro spoke to Grit to console them. 'Don't worry, everything will be okay. They won't hurt us as long as we cooperate.'

The soldiers took Grit and Gabbro to a League Surveillance Outpost, a building camouflaged into the landscape. The two Insurrectionists were thrown into a cell, its metal door almost like an airlock. A slam filled the air, then silence.

Gabbro tries to console Grit once more. 'Are you okay? Feeling alright?'

'Yeah, I'm fine.' Grit answers in a sore tone.

Scanning the cell, Gabbro spoke aloud softly. 'Secure containment. Looks like we'll be here a while.'

Out of all the thoughts buzzing around in Grit's head, one stood out. It became very clear—scary, even. Grit built up the courage to ask, 'How do you know that?'

Gabbro stops in his tracks, looking directly at Grit as they let out an admission.'Beca use... I used to work for the League. I managed to... escape, and now they've found me.'

Grit felt outrage course through them. *How long has Gabbro been lying to me? Are they a killer too? How can I trust a killer?*

-Part 4-

Grit spoke, trying to conceal their anger. 'How long have you been lying to me?'

Gabbro's head sank. They look up at Grit, imploring. 'Can you just let me explain what happened?'

'How long have I trusted a killer?' Grit began to tear up. Their best friend worked for The League. The organisation has a hit list of innocent people who had been infected with the Virus against their will. It wasn't *their* fault they had dangerous superpowers.

Gabbro's voice was low, pleading. 'I don't work for the League anymore. I couldn't after I realized what they were doing to people. You have to understand; I'm not one of them.'

'But you used to be, didn't you?' Grit's conclusions disgusted them.

Gabbro was desperate to explain. 'I couldn't lie to you, even about this. But I never wanted to look back to the monster I was. I'm sorry I hid it from you.'

Grit's tears began to run. They sat down in a corner of the cold metal cell. Gabbro approaches Grit and begins patting their back to comfort them. Grit pulls away in anger as Gabbro moves back to sit beside Grit.

'Even if you don't trust me, I will still get us out of here.'

Grit sobs, anguish lacing their tears. 'But... I thought you could only climb walls?'

Gabbro holds out their hand. A small ripple of light moves out from the centre of their palm, radiating to the edges. Grit moves back in surprise. The light grew out of Gabbro's hand, heat radiating from it.

'Picked up a few tricks fighting a League member when I quit. All we have to do is wait until at least one of the airlock doors is open, then I can just about manage melting one open, and we escape.'

Grit gave a nod. Maybe Gabbro was truly an Insurrectionist. After waiting for a while, Grit finally asks, 'How did you... quit?'

Gabbro snorts softly. 'Well, I didn't quit, I escaped. I was on a mission to take out a superhuman called Metalhead, with another League member named Pyrolysis, who had fire powers. We arrived at a harbour where spies told us Metalhead would be and waited.

I heard footsteps so I told my associate to get ready to ambush. We jumped out to attack and...'

Gabbro pauses for a moment as Grit urges them to continue. Sadness crossed Gabbro's face as they continued. '... Metalhead was a mother. A poor mother with powers that The League thought may be dangerous. I couldn't bring myself to attack her. Pyrolysis and Metalhead fought, shrapnel and fire going everywhere. I stood between them. 'Don't hurt her!' I had yelled. But I was pushed aside. Metalhead was assassinated.'

'That's terrible!' says Grit. The League was truly evil for all they had done.

'Well, I was next, I guess. By standing in the way of the League, I had been deemed a threat. Pyrolysis began shooting fire at me. I dove into the water of the harbour to escape, but by then the heat had left me with some burns. In the following months, I had been hunted by Pyrolysis. After some time, The League must have thought I had deceased, so they removed the hit. About then, I joined The Insurrectionists.'

Grit took all this in. Pyrolysis is still out there. Gabbro says to Grit, 'After all that, I'm glad I could mentor someone like you.'

Grit smiles.

-Part 5-

It had been hours in the cell, but finally, it was dinner time. And that meant that Grit and Gabbro could escape. The outer door opens, a symphony of screeches. Gabbro began using Pyrolysis's ability of fire to heat the door. As Gabbro's palm touches the door, the metal begins to melt. In a matter of seconds, the door was gone. Grit and Gabbro jump forward to ambush the LeagueMember. To their surprise, it was none other than Mockingbird.

'*What are you doing here*?'Shouts Grit in alarm. Did Mockingbird work for The League too?

'I'm here to rescue you. And Gabbro too, I guess. Cannoneer is outside; let's go.'

The three ran out of the cell. Gabbro asks as they run, 'How did you find us?'

'When we looted the tower, I found out about this Surveillance outpost. You and Grit went missing, so we figured The League took you here,' Mockingbird replies.

Cannoneer joins them as they escape. All four of them race toward the Insurrectionist's sanctuary. Upon reaching their home, Grit thanks Mockingbird and Cannoneer for their help, and joins Gabbro.

'Hey, I just wanted to say, thank you,' says Grit.

Gabbro looks confused. 'You're welcome, but for what exactly?'

'For changing. Even if it wasn't easy or instant, you changed for the better. Thanks.'

Gabbro smiled. 'No worries, buddy.'

The End.

THE ROAD OF ROT

DAMIEN DAVIS

In a place unknown, there was a kingdom, now a pathetic pile of debris of concrete and the dead. From a building upon its side, in the outer corners of the ruins, an odd flash of red light occurred. Out came a strange man; the Scribe, his face and body covered, a reticule in his right hand, and two long pieces of rolled-up paper upon his back.

He surveyed the landscape briefly, the red sky like the blush of an angry drunk and the black ground like ash; random pools of dried blood along the road, pointing towards the tower in the distance that seemingly breached the clouds in its size and stature. The Scribe began to walk down this dilapidated road, walking on and over piles of debris.

Then another thing appeared—unlike the dead that littered the exposed innards of the buildings that once stood so tall, this 'person' was very much alive. A reedy voice echoed from its maw.

'Who are you, dear stranger?' they asked.

The Scribe stood, unperturbed by the strange creature that stood before him, its long arms keeping the scraps of cloth to its frail body, its drawnhood not revealing what lurked underneath. But from what could be seen by the Scribe, its skin was like that of raw pork in both colour and most likely texture.

The stoic voice of the Scribe echoed in the otherwise silent environment.

'My name is not of importance. Refer to me by title—I am the Scribe.' His singular red eye glared at the figure who stood eight feet tall, even though the thing was hunched.

'Is your name that of Sock? Are you embarrassed?' the figure asked as it began chuckling. 'Or is that mask of yours just for show? Either way, I respond not to mere titles, so unless you say otherwise, Sock shall be your name.'

The Scribe let out a sigh.

'Fine, so be it.' He then sat on a large piece of debris, putting his reticule to the side and taking out its contents: a vintage typewriter.

'As you know, I am a Scribe; we make documents and—'

'Yes! Yes! I know what a Scribe is!'

'—I interview those in dying places, and write it all down; now may I ask, what is your name? If you have one, of course.'

The creature wearily crouched on the bare ground, which looked awkward, as she was still hiding her form from view with the scraps she seemed to refuse to leave behind.

'Very well then Sock, I'll relent. My name is Margret, Margret Turre.'

The Scribe quickly put paper in his typewriter and began furiously typing. The noise of the machine echoed in the stagnant silence.

'Now Margret, I thank you for your cooperation. What did you do? For work, I mean.'

'The King's personal maid.' Margret seemed to stare past the Scribe, as if reminiscing, 'But then he caused the red rot, and the ex-lord becoming a catalyst for a coup.' She took off her hood and revealed her face, a mass of silver eyes all with long lashes. However, a long scar breached her bulbous head, revealing a large cave of gnashing, grinding bone.

'One of the traitorous rats did this to me; praise the God of Dust, I didn't get red rot.'

The Scribe stopped typing.

'What did you say?' the Scribe asked.

'Uncultured too, so predictable,' Margret muttered. 'The God of Dust, dear Sock, is the great being who runs all things: "he is the King of Dust. He is above the King of Dust and the God of Dust is below the King"; The Book of Thieves one, four and—'

The Scribe gave yet another irritated sigh. 'Yes, yes, I know of it, surely you haven't read the eight Books of Dust?'

'Hark! All eight? I've read all eight a million times over! The Book of Thieves, The Book of Fools, The Book of Sins, The Book of Moon, The Book of Ash, the Book of

Creation, The Book of Keys, and The Book of Blood; all of which I have memorised and etched into my eyes! For that is the law of our holy land!'

The Scribe stopped typing, his hands shaking, his breaths shallow and empty.

'Are you alright?' Margret asked, shambling her way towards the Scribe.

The Scribe shivered.

'Yes, yes, I am alright.' The Scribe began typing again.

'Now, what do you do know?

'Crush the rats' heads.' When she uttered this sentence, her words were a ghost, distant, and empty. 'Just like the King had instructed of me.' Margaret began shifting on the ground. The Scribe took the transcript out from the typewriter.

'Thank you for your compliance.' The Scribe carefully rolled up the barely filled-in piece of paper and then put the typewriter into his reticule. Margret rose to her feet.

'That's all?' she asked, seemingly irritated.

'Yes, now goodbye.'

The Scribe began walking briskly towards the towers in the distance. The sound of ticking followed the Scribe as he moved.

Further down the path, he saw a Goliath in great armor, a being of immense stature. Dead and decrepit, it rested itself on a crumbled wall. It had an equally colossal axe lodged in its face. The Scribe looked at the weapon covered in blood. The Scribe quickly faced the straight road he walked.

'Who is making that confounded ticking sound?' he yelled.

Nobody answered.

With a huff, the Scribe walked onwards, past the Goliath and past fallen rubble. After an hour of travel, consistently interrupted by that damned ticking, the Scribe was a mere thirty minutes away from the great tower. Next to him was a large building, one of the few that were not destroyed.

It was of great height; not close to the height of the tower ahead, but still great in stature compared to the common construction. He wandered inside; the interior was that of worship, and three statues of the Trinity of Dust sat proudly in the centre on their respective thrones. The King of Dust with his long beard and great crown, the rubies for his eyes gleaming in the relative darkness. Next to him was the fair Meredith; her head was that of her own foetus, with its umbilical cord connected to her neck. Behind both was a large pile of stone. The God of Dust. It would have been almost perfect, if it weren't for the dead body suspended from the rafters.

It was a pontiff; she had a black gown with black roses and vines that reached to a point like a hat on her head. The sides of her head were covered with a material that was connected to the rest of her outfit, which along with her long slender gloves, made only her face visible. She had horns that reached forward from her head, with a mouth that opened sideways, revealing a cavern of razor-sharp teeth.

The Scribe looked around; apart from the pews, there was nothing of interest.

He walked out of the building and as he did, he heard something.

Like that of someone breathing. . .

He turned. There, in that building in the shadows, a thing sat, right in the furthest pew. That infernal ticking was as loud as ever, Tick, tock, tick, a mocking tensing of the mind. He couldn't quite make it out, though he could tell it was tall. *Very* tall. With a singular red eye that burned through his eyelids into his soul. It had multiple things on its side, attached to it with rope. They might have been plates, but the Scribe couldn't tell.

'Who are you?' The Scribe asked as he walked towards, each step a cry to run away echoing in his mind. The creature then seemingly vanished, a mockery of his question. The Scribe blinked once and it was there, and now, it was gone. He stared at that empty place. The Scribe shook his head.

He continued onward, approaching the tower. Between him and it was a bridge that overlooked a river. But there was someone on that bridge. He was five feet, slightly shorter than the Scribe. Their clothes were fine, and in their hands was a simple fishing rod, and next to them was a bucket of squirming bait. He turned to the Scribe.

'Good morning.' The figure's mouth made a kind of popping sound, and their mouth was caved in, the lips and the skin underneath covering their teeth. Their eyes were no different.

The Scribe nodded.

'Good morning, what is your name?' the Scribe stood next to the albino figure.

'Prince Olaf.' The Royal put some bait on their hook and threw it into the water. The Scribe sat down, taking out his typewriter, inserting a new piece of paper into the platen.

'Who are you, stranger?' Olaf asked.

'You can call me the Scribe.'

The Prince nodded and began propping up the fishing line against the rail. 'Well then, Mr. Scribe, I advise you to leave the kingdom. It isn't as glorious as it once was if you haven't noticed. Besides, there is nothing here for you anyway.'

The Scribe shook his head.

'People like you are the reason I came here, your Highness; I document the thoughts of people in dying places.'

'I see. I suppose you want to talk to me too?' The Prince turned to the river below, the grimy waters failing to reflect anything.

'What did you do Olaf?'

'Fishing— lots and lots of fishing.' The Prince motioned towards the fishing rod. The Scribe began vigorously typing into his typewriter, a sound at war with that seemingly unending ticking.

'What about your royal responsibilities?' The Scribe asked, their redeye peering deep into the Prince's caved-in eyes.

'The King decided that I was an omen, and you don't give an omen duties, let alone royal ones.' The Prince pointed to the large holy building that the Scribe had recently entered.

'I wasn't allowed in the Royal Tower and had to stay within the Holy Chapel with Pontiff Magdalene. I suppose you saw her earlier?' The Scribe nodded. 'I believe the King had her killed there. I think it was after she broke her holy oath and exposed Lord Duncan's plan to take over the Kingdom and marry the Queen.' The Prince pointed towards a small patch of land in the lake in the distance. 'That's where she wanted to be buried.'

'I see,' the Scribe said. The Ticking grew louder, a monolithic barrage of sound. 'Do you have any idea where that damned ticking is coming from?'

The Prince shook his head.

'I don't know what you are talking about, Scribe. I do not hear any such thing.'

The Scribe stood up. 'You don't hear anything? Nothing at all?' The ticking never wavered. A menace upon the Scribe's mind, 'I-I suppose not. . . I must be. . . mistaken.' The Scribe sat back down. 'So, what are you looking to catch?'

Olaf stood there; after a moment, he seemed to reanimate.

'I seek a golden carp.' The Prince looked down into the water. 'I believe it is the last fish in this lake... I apologise, Scribe but I would rather be left alone now.'

'Very well.'

The Scribe stood up once more and walked towards the great tower.

The Ticking didn't stop. It was like a vulture following someone they believe will die. The Scribe eventually found himself in front of two massive doors of iron, slightly rusted and heavily dented. Two impenetrable walls stood high on either side of the gate. The Scribe slipped past the small opening between the two doors.

He found himself in a garden. It was full of weeds and the plants that remained were overgrown. The Scribe began to head towards his destination: the large tower that was surrounded by the unkempt flora. The Scribe froze, his breathing heavy.

There was movement in the tall weeds, The Ticking seemed almost ecstatic. Then its face rose above the plants. Half of it was visible; the rest was covered by a fragment of the mask of buskin. A red eye behind its mask stared directly at The Scribe. Its other side was made of pork-like flesh. Instead of an eye, a clock was in its socket, and multiple mouths were on its head—one on the top, one on the side, and the other on the bottom. From the top and side were tongues connected to hourglasses. The Scribe began running to the tower's entrance. He got to the door and slammed it shut, resting against the door after the fact. The Ticking seemed to have faded away...

The Scribe let out a shaky sigh and began to look around at the gilded environment. Three halls led to three rooms. In the centre was a spiral staircase with ornate marble carvings of the wind on the handrails. The Scribe looked upwards. The staircase kept going on and on as if it was unending.

The Scribe began to check every room. Most were empty rooms for maids and other paid servants, while other rooms were lavish and filled with trinkets. Others had more personal items, such as family pictures, letters— even papers of accomplishments such as academic certificates, and military badges of honor. But all of them were absent of people. Every second floor had a kitchen in the middle door filled with ovens, mortars, knives, and other cooking equipment.

After around the thirty-ninth floor, the floors seemed to become even more glamorous, with precious metals in abundance and fine artistry of paintings and sculptures, normally of religious significance; one of which was a figure with a sword raised high towards the last floor. On the fortieth floor, instead of three hallways, there was one large door that was directly in front of the stairway, almost completely covered in precious metals and gems. The Scribe began to open the door. The insides of the room were that of a grand throne room, and it mirrored the extravagance of the door. Except it was of utter depravity. Upon the King's throne was a wooden post. With four planks nailed at the top of the post, the planks were all angled upwards, but the worst part was the corpse on it.

Their jaws were ripped off and their forehead was nailed directly into the post. Their arms were severed, and their elbows were nailed to the ends of the angled planks. They had been gutted with their insides on full display. Although some of their organs were missing... The Ticking rejoiced and began to release its blasphemous cry. The sound of heavy metal boots hitting the stairs was almost completely muffled. The Scribe turned to the sound, from the stairway in the corner stood a knight in broken armor. Their sword was unsheathed.

'State your purpose here.' His voice was akin to a bass drum, booming and dripping with authority. The Scribe looked at The Knight.

'I-I am the S-scribe; I document those in dying places.'

The Knight scoffed in response.

'Leave now! You are not wanted here!' The Scribe backed up to the doorway. The Knight stomped towards him, his sword gleaming directly into his red eye.

The Scribe descended the stairs in a rush as if to mimic the tempo of the Ticking that seemed to echo directly in their ears. Stumbling to his knees at the end of the stairway, the Knight still followed behind, keeping watch from a distance.

'I'm sorry, I can't go, I saw something. . . horrible, right outside the door.' The Scribe murmured, pointing towards the entrance.

The Knight let out a huff. 'You will leave now! Horror or not. The King's Tower remains vacant.'

The Knight descended the remaining stairs with many dull thuds, aiming their sword at The Scribe's throat. Its iron reflected menacingly in the dim light. With a sudden burst of energy, The Scribe ran past The Knight, a sharp hot pain in his side as the blade cut through his robes like butter. He scrambled upwards, The Knight in pursuit.

At the top of the floor, the Scribe turned and shoved as hard as his muscles would allow, the Knight stumbled backward falling off the stairway and directly upon the sword of the statue underneath. At the sickening sound of sliced flesh, The Ticking became louder still, omnipresent in its volume and ferocity. From behind him, the Scribe saw the figure, half the mask of Buskin, with crimson robes and a scythe made of paper. Clocks hung from its body and clothes. The Scribe descended the bottom of the stairs as fast as he could.

Breathing shakily as he did. He barged through the door and ran towards the bridge where he saw Olaf, their head completely submerged in the lake's water.

He wasn't moving.

The Scribe ran to the chapel and closed the heavy doors behind him. He sat in front of the statues and prayed for forgiveness. The Scribe could hear Buskin behind him, its breath freezing his neck. He turned facing the blade of the fiend. The Scribe took out from their pocket a measly pocketknife and aimed it at the creature. The Buskin reached out a hand and swiftly gripped the knife, the blade in its hand. Blood began to spill from The Scribe's hand. The Buskin then lifted the blade to its neck and sliced through it.

The Scribe fell to the floor, his own knife embedded into his neck, his blood joining the soil and those who had once lived on that land.

THE YEOMAN'S ESCAPE

MIKHAEL CROSSFIELD

The cell was dark and damp.

In one corner of the cell was a rathole in which now and then, a rat would come out and scuttle around the cell. The only light infiltrating the space was a few holes in the roof of the cell. The musky stench of past prisoners filled the air of the dark, damp cell.

As for the prisoner, his only thoughts were of trying to escape this grim place and praying to the gods for inspiration. It was about in one of those moments that he heard the stomping of multiple sets of boots coming closer to his cell.

'Someone wants to have a few words with you, mate,' said one of the guards.

The prisoner heard the clink of keys as another guard pulled a key out, opening the cell gate. He then approached the prisoner and squatted down to his level.

'It's best to be on your best behaviour, mate. Because if you're not, things will get ugly, real fast,' said the other guard.

The prisoner turned his head and gave a blank look.

'I'm not afraid; I've been and seen a lot worse,' said the prisoner.

'You will be soon enough,' replied the guard.

At that exact moment, another guard appeared. He also went into the prisoner's cell, grabbed him under the arms, and dragged him out. The prisoner wanted to fight back, but he was too weak. *There has to be a way out; if only I had my short sword, this would be no problem,* thought the prisoner. They dragged him along, eventually coming to a large door, one of them banged on the door and demanded to be let in.

The guard on the other side of the door looked through a hole. When he noticed the prisoner, he opened it with great haste. The guards, still dragging the prisoner, went to the middle of the room, dropping the prisoner on the floor. The prisoner looked up and saw devices that were used for torture. The room was lit up with what looked like a hundred candles, added to the details were also a few dead bodies that had not survived interrogation. A cloaked figure entered the light and squatted down to the prisoner's level, looking at him with curiosity.

'Well, well, well. If this one's survived this long, how long do you think he'll last under interrogation?' chuckled the cloaked figure.

'A lot longer than you think,' said the prisoner. He still had enough spirit to look at the cloaked figure and smirk.

'Spirited, I like that; more fun for me. No matter, when I'm done with you, you'll be begging me to kill you,' replied the cloaked figure.

"You won't be able to pull off what you're doing; even the Cai'ranians would know you're unleashing the seven hells,' said the prisoner.

The cloaked figure walked towards the prisoner and croaked in his ear, 'That's the idea.'

The prisoner's eyes widened and realised what the cloaked figure's intentions were. 'You're mad!'

The cloaked figure smirked. 'Guards, leave us!'

He then walked away from the prisoner, positioning himself in front of his victim. Next, he pulled out from underneath his tunic what appeared to be an uncut piece of a large, morganite gem.

What is he doing? No! How? His gaze widened in shock as the cloaked figure started to speak in a dialect of elvish.

'Let's begin, where did you hide the three orbs?'

'Somewhere you will never find them,' the prisoner ground out.

The cloaked figure shot a sinister look; he was clearly not in the mood for playing games. Extending his hand, a pulse of magical energy came out. The prisoner was shocked; what he saw were threads of various colours, like a rainbow. The threads then started to weave around the prisoner's throat, arms, and legs.

'Who taught you how to weave the arcane veil? Only the elves know how to weave at this level.'

The cloaked figure simply grinned as he finished the spell and then triggered a pulse of magic energy. The prisoner let out a gasp as he felt the magic threads strangle his throat as he was being lifted into the air.

'Firstly, do not try my patience; secondly, answer the question,' he snarled.

The prisoner was trying to find the words, but the constant gasping made it difficult to put together a sentence. 'Who...in...the... seven hells...are...you?' He let out another gasp of air and at the same time, felt his arms and legs being stretched. The tug slackened as the figure released the prisoner from his magic vice.

'Very well; I will show you since your fate is sealed.'

He lowered his hand and then pulled back the hood to reveal a head of thinned short snow white hair. The left eye had a white iris, the other green; a scar ran over his left eye. His skin had apapery texture like the elderly had, grey and translucent. Semi-rotten teeth grinned at him. He looked as if he was in his nineties but had an agile grace to his movements.

The prisoner then felt a sense of terror as if something had reached into and squeezed his chest. The breaths that he took were short and fast. 'No! That's impossible! You're supposed to be dead!'

'Dead? That is half true I suppose, but now I go by a different name,' the cloaked figure paused, 'I am now known as Abraxon.'

The prisoner attempted to find his footing while trying to make sense of the situation, confusion, and shock still in his mind and body. 'Let me guess, you outsmarted the other generals and killed them all?' The look that he gave Abraxon was one of unsurprise.

'Clever boy, but it had to be done,' said Abraxon. Abraxon then raised his hand, unleashing a pulse of magical energy that hit the prisoner. He started to raise him in the air.

The magic energy that Abraxon cast was more intense than the last time.

"Now let's try this again, where...are...*the orbs?*' growled Abraxon.

'Where...you'll...never find them!' The prisoner gasped. The intensity of the magical energy coming from Abraxonwas so severe that a trickle of blood came out of the prisoner's nose. Then out of nowhere, the locked door was kicked in, breaking Abraxon's concentration.

His attention now turned to the intruder; he launched a blast of magical energy as the intruder drew out a long, black blade and uttered some words. Abraxon's magic blast was reflected, knocking him off his feet, and releasing the prisoner, who fell to his feet and then his knees. His energy was almost completely drained. The intruder sheathed his blade, picking up the prisoner by placing his arm around his shoulders before dragging him out of the chamber.

'By the gods, mate, you're bloody heavy for a prisoner!' He continued to drag the prisoner through the hallway and up a flight of stairs; it was clear he was feeling the strain from carrying another person upward.

'Where...are...we going?' The prisonerpanted.

'Firstly, the guardhouse; they have the rest of my gear,' replied the intruder, struggling to keep his companion upright.

'The orbs...we need to get...orbs.'

There was noise coming outside of the building, and guards were running all over the place. They were near the main entrance, but the intruder was running out of strength from carrying the prisoner. They stopped outside a row of rooms for a pause. The intruder looked around and found a room that had an open door. With a grunt, he then dragged the prisoner inside and hid him in a closet that was near a bed.

'What are you doing?' Whispered the prisoner.

'Listen, the guardhouse is close. If I drag you with me, it's both our heads, so stay here.'

The intruder was just about to step outside of the room and close the door when he turned his head and noticed two guards coming down the hall. He immediately dashed back inside the room and hid behind the door where it swung inward. The steps grew louder and louder, then the noise stopped suddenly. One of the guards must have noticed that the door was open. He then peeked his helmeted head inside and looked left and right, then removed his head.

'Come on, I heard another guy escaped,' said the guard.

The other guard then closed the door, turned, and they both proceeded down the hall.

The intruder waited for a few beats, before before exhaling in relief. He opened the door slightly to make sure the guards were gone, snuck out, and went down the hall. After making it to the end, the intruder came to the massive main hall; holding up the roof were half a dozen pillars. The walls were grey but decorated with massive portraits of past commanders and rulers. The tables were long and carved with patterns with due care, surrounded by statues of enemies of the past.

As soon as he made it to the door, it burst open and it almost caught the intruder by surprise as he dived underneath one of the tables. He began to overhear a conversation that, judging by the glimpses of armour, was between a commander and his lieutenant.

'Has anyone located those orbs yet?' Boomedthe Commander.

'No, but we received word that an enemy soldier has been captured and they're interrogating him as we speak, Sir,' replied his lieutenant.

They continued walking down the main hall and down the corridor where the rooms were. *I better hurry, I'm running out of time,* thought the intruder as he scurried after them.

The doors that led to the courtyard were surrounded by massive ramparts that were lit up by torches that were carried by sentries, who were always watching. On one side there were horses strapped to a post so they would not escape the premises, and a courtyard also doubled as a training ground for he could see archery targets and battered training dummies.

He looked around and finally spotted the guardhouse near the tower's exit. It was large enough to hold at least three guards; some windows showed the inside, but there was no door so there was quick access in and out; everything had to be timed perfectly, for he knew the consequences of failure.

Meanwhile, the prisoner had regained a little strength from his rest Sluggish, he looked around and realised that he was in a closet full of clothes.

'How long was I out for?' He puzzled, voice gruff from the strangulation. Opening the closet doors to look at his surroundings, he noticed the simple bed and military clothes. 'I must be in a soldier's sleeping quarters. But wait, where is that man who freed me?'

He quickly removed his tattered clothes and replaced them with a soldier's uniform that was in the closet. Then he approached the door, opening it slightly to look in the hall; he could hear footsteps but couldn't see anyone.

Abruptly his vision was blocked, and the door he was using as cover was opened fully, hitting his face and causing him to fall back. Standing at the entrance was a commander and his lieutenant. The commander and the prisoner stared at each other for a second. The lieutenant, noticing that he was not part of the garrison, went to grab the imposter; however, the prisoner was slightly faster. He grabbed the lieutenant's cloak and threw the man over his head, pushing the lieutenant out of the way. The commander grappled the prisoner as he attempted to run. He had almost been successful, his big muscular arms wrapped around the prisoner's body, lifting him. The prisoner, however, by sheer luck, was able to free one of his arms and strike the commander with his elbow, causing himself to be dropped. The prisoner found his footing, stood up, and ran for the exit.

The prisoner didn't twice think about the sentries on the ramparts, or any guards on patrol as he sprinted down the corridor. He looked around for the intruder that freed him before, but just when he thought he was in the clear, he got stopped by a guard on patrol.

'Who are you?' Asked the guard.

'A transfer,' the prisoner said swiftly, a bead of sweat upon his brow. The guard looked at him with suspicion, then his eyes widened. That's when the commander and the lieutenant ran out into the courtyard.

'Sound the alarm, a prisoner has escaped!' shouted the commander.

One of the sentries heard the shouting coming from the courtyard nearby, looking around until he spotted the prisoner with the guard. All the other sentries then came running downstairs to the courtyard, some carrying torches, others carrying spears; a couple were armed with longbows, but they covered the rampart. The prisoner looked around and realised there was no escape.

While the guards, commander, and lieutenant surrounded the prisoner, their focus was interrupted by a loud *ka-boom*; a couple of the guards got blasted into the air, the initial shock confusing the surrounding party.

Smoke and dirt were flying everywhere; the guards, commander and lieutenant, and prisoner were running blind, they couldn't see anything. From the chaos came the intruder, who ran towards the prisoner, seizing him by the arm.

'What are you *doing*? Let's go!' hissed the intruder as he grabbed the prisoner by the hand and hurried him to the horses.

They nearly made it to the horses but were stopped by one of the sentries on the rampart who shot an arrow at them; the intruder took out a liquid-filled vial, and in it was a small crystal shard. He shook it furiously and threw it as hard as he could at the sentry above them; there was another resonating *ka-boom*, and the sentry was blasted from the rampart.

'What was that?' asked the prisoner.

The other guard saw the prisoner and the intruder. He was still getting over the shock of the blast as he took his bow and nocked an arrow. But when he tried to aim there was too much chaos in the courtyard; he caught a glimpse of the prisoner and took his shot.

He heard a groan from who he thought was the prisoner he shot at; however, when the smoke from the blast cleared from the courtyard, it was revealed to be one of the guards. The shooter's face went from pleasure to shock at what he had done.

The prisoner and intruder unstrapped the horses, mounted them, and began making their way toward the closed gate; the intruder took out another explosive vial, shaking it furiously as they approached the barred gate, and threw it.

Ka-boom! The vial exploded as soon as it hit the massive door; all that was remaining was a massive hole. The prisoner and intruder bolted for the exit without any thought.

'Looks like you have some strength back in you, mate," laughed the intruder. The prisoner simply nodded as they both exited the courtyard, and the intruder was reminded about something the prisoner had told him about.

'By the way, these orbs you talk about, where are they?' he asked.

The prisoner simply said, 'Follow me.'

It took about half an hour to get to their destination.

It was a massive tower with a very unusual construction, as if was spiraling towards the sky. A mix of different cultures was put into building this tower. The prisoner started glancing around. The intruder was looking at the tower walls when he noticed the different colored bricks in the walls; those were the orbs that the cloaked figure and the prisoner were talking about.

Clever, thought the intruder.

He was very impressed by how he'd hidden the orbs right under the noses of his enemies; it didn't take long for the prisoner to finish what he was doing. He then mounted his horse, and they both left the way they came, unseen and silent.

It took the rest of the night, dodging enemy patrols, and taking regular stops to let the horses drink water from the river before the prisoner decided to ask for the intruder's name.

'I thought you'd never ask. Azmund von Ecclestein the second, but you can call me Azmund the Great Journeyman. And your name?'

"Ioan Valtrac, Imperial Yeoman to Lord Gaiseric of Val'tea", said Ioan, once prisoner.

Both were getting close to the Harbour, but then they got stopped by a group of soldiers; one cloaked in a dark purple uniform, one cloaked in green and light brown, and two soldiers clothed in what looked like a scout uniform.

'Well, I guess this is where we part ways, however, I owe you my life,' said Ioan.

Azmund replied, "If we meet again, you might find me at the Tempting Soul Tavern in Cimbra".

Ioan smiled, shook arms with Azmund, and then moved forward towards the soldiers; Azmund looked at the group for a few moments, then galloped away.

'Who was that?' asked one of the soldiers; Ioan turned his behind him and merely replied, 'A friend.'

The purple-cloaked man walked up to Ioan and said, 'We can do the pleasantries later; for now, you have a lot of explaining to do.'

'Yes, indeed, Ta'ne,' replied Ioan. The group of soldiers then started to towards the harbour.

While they were walking, they saw something glowing yellow in the distance; the green-cloaked man then said, 'Liranais ablaze; I hope they cleared the library and the archives'.

'Mosi, I think that's the last thing we need to think about', said Ioan.

'What could be more important?' replied Mosi.

Ioan pulled out the bag that had the three orbs in it; he then brought everyone up to speed on what had happened.

'Very well, then we need to work fast,' said Ta'ne.

When they finally reached the harbour, the group unloaded their things into the boat and sailed back to Val'tea. Ioan, Ta'ne, and Mosi realised this was just the beginning of something bigger than they imagined.

Dragonspeaker

Milla Adams

The forest was loud today. The weather was clear with nothing to muffle or distort the sounds, and last night's rain had stirred all the creatures of the forest.

Including her.

Lienne glided through the undergrowth, rich with life and variety. Her tail trailed behind her, curling through the thick covering of litter. On days like this, it was best to sound like one of the various small mammals and reptiles foraging the damp leaves for worms and bugs brought to the surface by the moisture seeping into the earth. She liked days like this, days where she could hear the whole forest.

She also liked how easy it was to hunt these days. All she had to do was stand still for long enough and prey would come to her. There was an assortment of snakes and lizards passing by, but she was feeling picky and decided to let them move on. It only took a few minutes before a flicker of movement caught her attention and she glanced over, spotting a young sparrow. Perfect. She subtly twitched the tip of her tail, enticing the bird to investigate what appeared to be a tasty bug. It got close enough for her to strike, but she didn't move. There was plenty of food in the forest and she wanted an easier catch, even if it meant giving the bird a chance at escape. Holding her tail still, so as not to distract the creature, she twitched her ear slightly, making the tuft of fur at the tip brush against the trunk of a tree. This again caught the sparrow's fleeting attention and it immediately hopped onto a branch, trying to spot the bug responsible. It never did. Within a flash of a second, Lienne's arm shot out, grabbing the bird. With a twist of her fingers, she snapped its neck before it even noticed anything was wrong.

Her prey fell limp in her hand, and she bit into it, spitting out the feathers. Fresh blood dripped over her lip, and she flicked out her tongue, also coated in blood, to lick it off. A pair of critterins came over to lap up the bloody feathers and bones she dropped in the leaves and bit off a leg to give them as well. Critterins were quite intelligent and could act as sentries for those they liked, so it was never a bad idea to drop them a bit of food now and then. Somehow, they always seemed to be aware of every little thing in the forest before even she was.

Except— a sound caught her attention, and she swiveled her ears to hone in on the cause. Footsteps. An intruder. She flicked her attention back to the critterins eating at her feet, seemingly unbothered by the threat. Lienne pulled back her ears and hissed in confusion and irritation, flicking her tail. She dropped her half-finished meal on the ground. She couldn't ignore a disturbance like this. Besides, the critterins would eat it, so it wouldn't go to waste. Although she was annoyed at having to abandon such a good catch for this, she didn't have time to eat it now, and she definitely didn't have the time to stash it in a way that would prevent scavengers from stealing it in her absence.

By the sounds of it, the intruder was slow, but somehow on a direct trajectory to the grove. Not good. Leaping into her treetops, she swiftly climbed to a nearby weapons stash. Grabbing a pair of daggers, she slashed at a gum tree, coating the blade with sap. She'd found that humans tended to react negatively when a little bit of sap got in their bloodstream. Pathetic. She usually finished them off before long-term effects were of any use, but she thought it would be better to play it safe with this one. It didn't sound quite like a human. Didn't really smell like one either. The scent was...warmer than a human's, or anything she'd encountered for that matter. There was less nuance to it as well, and it was quite strong. There was something else, too. It sounded smaller, but the scent was somewhat similar. The same warmth, but with a reptilian tone to it. Both were unlike anything she'd encountered before, and she kept her guard up as she stalked closer.

The first thing she noticed was its armour. It was thick leather, unusual for an attack scout, but not too noteworthy. What caught her attention, however, was the shape. Its arms and legs were almost completely exposed and there wasn't any back on the chest plate. Instead of armour, its limbs and part of its back were covered in small, golden-brown dots. Despite the obvious weaknesses of such low coverage, the design seemed intentional, due to the clean cuts and stitchings. The intruder was bulky and slow and seemed completely at ease with the human corpses strung through the branches at various stages of decomposition. This was rather annoying, as Lienne had put in a lot of work stringing them up for the sole purpose of scaring intruders. They were usually intimidated at the very least, but whatever this thing was, it barely spared a glance at her work.

The creature at its feet was strange too. Possibly a hunting dog, though it didn't look or act like the other dogs she'd seen. It smelt like a lizard but was about the size of a large badger, and much longer. It was covered in scales the colour of mud and had a pair of horns sprouting from its skull at a slight curve. A row of small spikes ran down its spine, seemingly undeveloped. Its tail swayed elegantly as it walked, but the effect was offset by a clumsy stride. Its paws and eyes looked strange, oversized as it stumbled through, letting out a chirp every few seconds.

What. . .what were they?

She flicked her ears with agitation, trying to shake off this growing sense of intrigue. Intruders were to die, no matter how mysterious. No, even more so if they were mysterious. She hissed. As soon as the sound left her mouth, her ears shot back and she froze. Straining against every panicked instinct to flee, she held herself still. If the intruders heard that and looked over, the slightest shift in position might give her away. This type of hunt was far better on a windy day, when noises blended together, and the forest moved more than enough to cover any slip-up. But the day was far too lovely. Still air carried and accentuated every sound and the motionless trees highlighted every twitch. Perfect weather to hunt—on both ends.

But the sound of the intruders didn't change. No pause in its stride or even the slightest hint in its heavy breathing to indicate that it had even heard her hiss, let alone try to pinpoint it. She slit open an eye, only to watch them walk straight past her. The creature at its feet was somehow completely unperturbed as well. Unlikely to be a hunting dog, then.

It might be better to play this one a little safer. Slipping through the trees with flowing grace, she raced for a poison stash. She would not let them slip through her claws. None had ever reached her grove and none ever would. She would kill them, had to kill them.

Here it was.

She pulled out a small bottle of her personal favorite blend. Unnamed as of yet, but one of her most potent concoctions. A delectable mix of strychnine berries, bracken sap, phantasmal frog poison, cortule berries, and daiman tree sap. All together making for a gorgeous neurotoxin that would kill in minutes. She rubbed a few drops over her knives, licking off the excess.

By the time she slipped back to the intruder, it was about halfway between the edge of the corpse forest and the stream that surrounded her grove. Farther than almost any other intruder had managed. Almost.

She didn't leap forward as soon as she usually would, mystery stilling her blade. What was this?

But… it didn't really matter. It was an intruder. It was heading for her grove. It was a threat.

Lienne bared her teeth, flexed her spurs impatiently, and tensed forwards. Waiting for it to step into her line of attack.

Almost.

Almost.

Almost.

NOW.

ROadTrip

Sonja Liszewski

Alt text:

Two people approach a house, a man and a woman. The man seeks to take a photo of the woman smiling in front of the house for their mother. He walks back, breaking something.

Alt text: They return to the car, wondering what was broken. They check the way to their destination, looking to arrive before lunch, when the sister notices a hooded figure outside the car.

Alt text: The sister comments that it's too hot for cloaks, with a concerned look on her face. The brother claims he doesn't see the figure at his sister's insistence.

Alt text: Noticeably upset, the sister stops the car to get out to look. The brother thinks she's joking, while she watches the hooded figure approach them.

Alt text: The sister yells to get back into the car as the figure approaches. They hurry back.

Alt text: the brother is frustrated he can't see the figure. The sister wants to know why it's following them and remembers it occurred after he knocked over the object earlier.

Alt text: they return to the house to repair the object, and see if it has any effect.

Alt text: they wait a while, and when they're sure, they head back on their way to their mother. Unfortunately, the comic ends with the hooded figure looming behind them.

DETECTIVE WHISPERER: THE SILVER MALLARD

Jaxon Devenport

My story begins at Wayville High School. The time is 3:19 p.m. on a Wednesday. School had now finished for the day, and I'd just started grabbing my things out of my locker—located in the hall just left of the main entrance—and was getting ready to head out. As I finished up and put my backpack on, I suddenly heard a low-volume, somewhat muffled, voice call out to me.

'Hey, Markus!' the voice said to me. At the same time, I looked down at my shirt pocket, noticing something moving around inside it. I immediately realised where that voice was coming from and who it was.

After quickly checking that no one was nearby, I leaned forward into my locker for some privacy—and to make sure nobody saw who, or more importantly, *what* I was talking to. I reached into my pocket, scooped him out, and placed him down in my locker. A small Deer Mouse crawled off my hand. Its soft brown fur, with a white under-belly, was well-groomed. This was my friend, partner, and pet mouse, Columbo; who I'd named after the homicide detective from the seventies crime show of the same title.

'So, I take it this means school's done for the day?' he asked, looking up at me.

'That's right!' I replied in a low tone, to avoid getting people's attention.

So, I guess now would be a good time to introduce myself. My name is Markus Richmond. I'm sixteen years old. I live with my mom, Liana, and my younger seven-year-old sister, Julia, in the riverside town of Wayville. It's located along the east side of the Tennessee River in Hardin County, along Cypress Slough, just north and opposite the river from Saltillo. And as you might have noticed by now, I can talk to animals; as in I can understand and converse with them, like Doctor John Dolittle, or Eliza Thornberry.

How is that possible? Well, to be completely honest with you, I have no idea myself. For as long as I can remember, I've always been able to do this. I remember when I was younger; I would regularly sit down in the front yard and have full conversations with the neighbour's dog all day, while everyone else didn't really think much of it, with me being just a child. I remember this one time when I was five, I almost gave Mom a heart attack when she saw me talking to Henry, the grizzly bear who lives in the woods north of town. I'm also pretty well known amongst the wildlife across the west half of Tennessee as 'the boy who can talk to animals'. Besides my sister, I've never really told anyone about my unique ability— and the last time I told my mother, back when I was seven, she just said I have an overactive imagination. But, besides all that, I've managed to live a pretty normal life so far.

That is, until about six months ago when a big key moment in my life unfolded.

There was an incident at my sister's elementary school. She was accused of stealing a silver pen from a classmate, who had gotten it as a birthday gift from his granny. They couldn't find the pen and had no solid evidence that she took it; but she was the one who'd bumped into the student and knocked over his things, leaving the pen nowhere to be found, making her the only potential suspect. However, while my mom and sister were in the principal's office, trying to sort things out, I was outside when I met Columbo for the first time. He told me that he saw who really took the pen, and thanks to him, I found the stolen pen in the real culprit's bag.

After that, I eventually decided to start using my ability to talk to animals to help people. After taking Columbo for a proper wash and full vet check-up, I took him in as my new pet. Now, with his help as my partner, I solve crimes around town under the alias of Detective Whisperer—it was a reference to me being a sort of animal whisperer. Which now brings me back to the story at hand.

'We've got a new case today, Columbo, and hopefully a relatively easy one,' I said as I reached into my bag and showed Columbo the front page of today's school newspaper issue. The headline read: **FAMILY HEIRLOOM STOLEN FROM LOCAL CAFÉ OWNER!**

'Mr. Irish's son, David, is a classmate of mine, so he told me everything first-hand. His family owns this life-sized statue of a Mallard duck made from pure silver, estimated to be valued at around eight hundred dollars. The police say they have a potential suspect, but so far have yet to take any action or announce any names, as usual. Let's start our investigation by grabbing some deets from our insider and find out who the suspect is.'

'All right, but I'll be waiting by the bike while you go talk to him. I hate the way he always stares at me with that hungry look in his eyes,' Columbo said in an annoyed, but assertive, tone.

Nodding in agreement with him, I slipped him back into my pocket, and we left the school. I unchained my bike and hopped on. Before heading off, I looked up towards the school clock tower stationed on top of the school. It said 3:22 p.m. My curfew on school nights was to be back home by five p.m. at the latest, giving us only an hour and a half to solve the case. Just for quick reference, by bicycle, it takes roughly ten to twelve minutes to ride from one side of town to the other.

With Columbo in my pocket, we rode south towards the Wayville Police station, located along the river shoreline in the mid-town area; but not before making a quick stop at the fish farm just two blocks north from the station. According to the station clock, it was 3:37 p.m. when we arrived. After chaining my bicycle to a lamp post, I made my way around the back of the station towards the back alley exit. As I got closer to the two-lidded dumpster by the door, I heard something moving, and then something leaped out from the open lid on the left, landing on top of the closed lid on the right.

On top of the dumpster was a male American Shorthair cat, whose fur was a black and bright brown colour pattern. It was Lupin, named after the gentleman phantom thief of French fiction by his owner, Officer Sabastian 'Sabie' Lockley—potentially the only actual good cop in town, making him my go-to cat for insider information on the force.

'So, What is it this time, detective?' asked Lupin in his usual done-with-everything tone of voice, with a clear hint of tiresomeness; as if he was just in the middle of napping, which, knowing him, was more than likely the case.

'I need a name,' I simply replied.

'Let me guess, the silver mallard case, right? Yeah, I heard Sabie complaining all day about the lack of public transparency with this one. They haven't even shared with the public that that's what was even stolen!' he said.

Now that I thought about it, the paper *did* say it was a family heirloom that was stolen, but it *didn't* mention what the heirloom in question was.

'I did hear mention of the name of a guy they suspect to be the culprit, given his track record.' Lupin started to roll onto his back like he was trying to find a comfortable resting position. 'Though it's strange; for some reason, I can't quite seem to recall what his name was...' His tone was a mixture of smug and sassy as he petted his belly two times with both his paws.

I've known Lupin for long enough to know by now that that was basically code for 'pay up' in cat--which is exactly why I stopped by the fish farm first. Reaching into my backpack, I pulled out a small, plastic, air-sealed bag containing a single Bluegill, just big enough to be within regulation. Bluegills aren't exactly cheap in our local market, but they're also Lupin's favourite type of fish. I took it out of the bag, holding it by the tail fin, and placed it down in front of him. Lupin then got back up on his paws and walked up to inspect the fish, eyeing it head to fin like... well, like a cat. After a moment, a small but noticeable smile formed on his lips, a clear sign he was happy with the quality.

'Kurt Nolin,' he simply said, looking back up to me. 'The suspect's name is Kurt Nolin. As for who that is? I've got nothing,' He added, before looking back down, holding down the fish by the head and fin with his paws, and taking a bite out of the middle.

'Kurt Nolin... got it! Holmes should be able to tell us more. Thanks, Lupin, see you around,' I said, heading back to my bike. 'Got what we needed!' I exclaimed, looking down at Columbo, who had been waiting beside my bike. I placed him back in my pocket, and we got moving.

As I arrived at the south edge of town, I asked a bystander if he had the time. He said it was now 3:44 P.M. After chaining my bike to a tree, I walked further into the southern woods, over to another much larger and thicker tree, and began my climb up the branches. While making my ascent, I could hear all the birds in the area chatting amongst each other. As it turns out, most birds are complete chatterboxes, and when it comes to topics of conversation, they don't exactly have the longest attention span. Birds can change the subject in seconds. One second, they'll talk about someone's new puppy, and then the next second, they'll talk about a burglary they saw last week; and then the *next* second, they'll talk about the new ice cream stall over in the park, and then the second after *that* they'll talk about someone plotting to poison the river—though thankfully, that was not based on a real example.

Because of this, it's nearly impossible for me to make any sense of what they're talking about. Fortunately, I know someone who *could* make sense of them. I stopped my climb at around one-third of the tree's total height and laid down on a branch where, just above the branch at the base of the tree, was a hole as big as the branch was thick.

'Holmes. . .? You home?' I called out, looking into the hole.

Before long, a large white owl stepped out of the tree hole and looked at me. It was my bird friend, Holmes, whose namesake, I think, is pretty obvious.

'Ah, Detective Whisperer; oh, and Columbo! It is always a pleasure to see you two.' He said in his usual happy, properly worded, and elderly tone. I don't know exactly how old he is, but it is clear from his voice that he's exceptionally old for an owl. 'So, what do you need to know today?' He asked.

'It's good to see you too, Holmes. There was a burglary last night, and I need some information on the prime suspect.'

'Ah, then you have come to the right place! What is the name of the suspect?'

Before responding, I looked away from him towards the neighbouring birds and said 'Kurt Nolin!' loud enough for the birds to hear.

There was a brief silence before the chatter picked up again. William the Blue Jay started up the chatter with, 'Hey, isn't that the human who...' and it was all immediately indistinguishable from there. At least, to me, it was. Holmes, on the other hand—or wing?— was listening in with a look of focus in his eyes.

Do you know how pop culture media often portrays owls as super smart-eggheads? Well, as someone who's got one for a friend *and* can understand him, I can tell you first-hand that it's completely accurate! And thanks to his impressive hearing skills, he's able to selectively listen out for specific topics among all the other birds and put the different sentences together to get the full picture. There is nothing that gets past him if the birds are talking about it.

'They are saying that Michael the Racoon spotted Mr. Nolin last night when he snuck into a closed café, and he came out holding something shiny that resembled a duck in appearance. Mr. Nolin was also seen this morning by Francine the Hawk, entering the pawn shop on the east side of town with a shiny duck in his arms, but when he left the shop, he was instead holding multiple pieces of green paper sheets.'

'It Sounds like he pawned off the silver mallard this morning,' exclaimed Columbo, poking out of my pocket.

'Agreed. In that case, we better go find David and make a trip to the pawn shop. Thanks, Holmes. I appreciate it!' I said, climbing back down.

'Please, the pleasure is all mine, Detective,' he replied, before retreating into his den.

It was now 4:15 P.M. by the time I found David and had him agree to come with me to the pawn shop. I figured it would be a good idea to bring along someone who can confirm whether it is the heirloom.

'So, how did you find it?' David asked me as we stepped into the pawnshop, a small bell ringing as the door swung open. I knew he would ask me sooner or later, so I'd taken some time to think of a cover-up. After all, it's not I can just tell him a cat told me, and an owl confirmed it.

'I was riding my bike around the area when I stopped for a quick break just outside the shop, and I noticed that silver duck statue through the glass,' I lied, pointing towards the silver duck in question, by the window sill.

'Oh, hello, Mr. Richmond, Mr. Irish! What brings you here today?' The shop owner, Rupert Travis, as he walked away from the counter. To this day, I still don't understand why he insists on addressing all of his customers as a Mr. or Mrs., even in cases where he's older than them, as was the case with me and David.

'Hi, Mr. Travis,' I greeted back. 'Um, out of curiosity, where did you get that silver duck statue?' I asked, pointing to it while David walked over and picked it up for a closer inspection.

'Hm? Oh, that? It, uh... a man stopped by and sold to me this morning. It's made from real silver, and he offered to sell it for four hundred bucks, even though I weighed it to be twice that. He seemed satisfied with only going for four hundred, though. Why do you ask?'

His story did add up with the evidence. Rupert got it at four hundred when its full value is double, as stated in the paper, and he said a man brought it here this morning, which matched up with Holmes' timetable. Now I just needed to see if Lupin's intel matched up, too, and ask for the seller's name. Before I could, however, David suddenly stepped forward, the silver mallard in hand.

'Yep! It's my family's heirloom, alright!' he announced as he pointed underneath the statue to something engraved on the bottom. 'This is my great grandfather's signature! He was a prospector back in the early days of this town, and this large vein of pure silver was his prized possession. He sold it to make his fortune, but kept this chunk of it and carved it into a duck,' He explained. 'Mr. Travis, I'm afraid this statue was stolen from my parents and pawned off to you. You can call them right now, and they'll tell you the same thing. But first, I need you to tell me: who sold it to you?' he demanded of Rupert.

'Oh!... uh... I believe it was Mr. Nolin...' he said.

'Bingo!' I heard Columbo whisper from my pocket.

Over the following forty-five minutes, David's parents confirmed his story, and after a quick call to the police, Kurt Nolin was promptly arrested at the local grocery store. With the heirloom back in its rightful place, Columbo and I declared the case closed and called in the day.

It was 4:58 P.M. when Columbo and I made it back home after I finished up with police questioning—with just two minutes to spare before my curfew deadline.

As I opened the front door and stepped inside, I yelled out, 'I'm home!'

'Welcome home, sweetie. You're just in time for dinner!' My mom yelled back from the kitchen. It smelled like she was cooking salmon. Yum!

'Big bro!' said my sister, Julia, as she ran up to hug me, which I happily obliged. 'So, what did you and Columbus do today?' she asked, as I could hear Columbo making an annoyed grumble from being misnamed. He didn't dislike Julia—far from it—but it was annoying to him that she kept misunderstanding his name. And besides, she's only seven; I'm sure she'll get it right eventually.

'Eh, just a simple stolen goods case, nothing particularly interesting. Anyway, come on, sis, let's enjoy some dinner together,' I said.

The End.

HOW STAR WARS BECAME MY OBSESSION

Bryce Noble

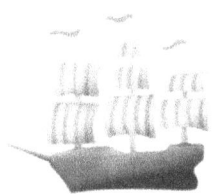

Star Wars is a Space Fantasy, Space Opera, and one of the biggest franchises in history.

For the longest time, I didn't have much interest in it. The Sequel Trilogy was interesting individually but struggled overall to land due to a lack of planning.

Enter Dave Filoni. He wrote Star Wars: The Clone Wars and Star Wars: Rebels and was well-known and respected among fans. In a time of darkness after the Sequel movies, Dave Filoni came to the rescue with The Mandalorian. And in the process, he lit the fire that would become my obsession with the Star Wars franchise.

I loved the story of Din Djarin and Grogu, the Baby Yoda. With Jon Favreau helping Dave Filoni, the story was gripping, epic, and awesome. Seasons two and three of *The Mandalorian* were also epic, and the story arc around Bo Katan was fascinating to see—even if Season three was affected by the cancellation of *Rangers of the New Republic*. My interest in *Star Wars* remained an interest as the Pandemic rolled around in 2020. As my *Pokémon* obsession continued, my *Pokémon* story would eventually conclude at a word count that totalled ninety percent of the *Lord of the Rings* trilogy word count.

In 2021, two factors accelerated my interest in *Star Wars* to an all-out obsession. The first factor was when I got a copy of the *Legends Thrawn Trilogy: Heir to the Empire, Dark Force Rising,* and *The Last Command.* I loved the entire story and finally understood how Mara Jade and Thrawn came into the franchise, and why they're so popular among fans. Honestly, Thrawn became one of my favourite characters in *Star Wars,* as I enjoyed his Sherlock Holmes-like skills in his war against the New Republic.

The other factor was *Star Wars: The Bad Batch.* And yes, the characters are a bit archetypal, and we're getting more than a few parallels between Grogu and Omega, and Din Djarin and Hunter; but the effects *Star Wars: The Bad Batch* had on me were profound. Not only was this story great to follow, but the fandom is also relatively small but magnificent, and thanks to a mix of prompting fanfiction writers, a writing mentor, and practising writing the characters, I improved the quality of my writing by a significant margin.

My favourite moment from *Bad Batch* Season Two is from Episode Nine when Omega and Tech are talking about adapting and moving with the times after Echo left to join Rex, where Tech implies he is on the Autism spectrum. I found this incredibly validating, as someone who has headcanoned Tech being on the Autism spectrum since the first Season. Speaking of the Autism spectrum, a popular headcanon that I agree with is that Omega is also on the Autism spectrum—specifically, how Autism usually manifests in females as opposed to males.

As to the future, I'm curious to see if the writers go down the route of Omega and possibly Hunter being force-sensitive, and how it ties into other series like *The Mandalorian, Ahsoka*—and even the Sequel Trilogy that the *Mandalorian* has started tying things into. Considering that in The Mandalorian Season Three, the project involving Darth Sidious had made little to no progress, potentially the Zillo beast will contribute to destroying the Mt. Tantiss facilities during *Bad Batch* Season Three. Are Omega and Hunter Force Sensitive in my headcanon? No. I headcanon their abilities are easily mistaken for Force Sensitivity—even if *Ahsoka* brought back the concept of everyone being capable of using the Force that George Lucas had first discussed during the Original Trilogy, but got lost at some point.

Also, let's address the final thing. Is Tech alive after the events of the last episode of Season Two? I could go either way. Although, in both cases, the writers must do a lot of writing and explanation. And, if Tech is dead, kill off Phee during Season Three to add an extra gut punch to Tech's demise. Also, Cid will work for the Empire whether or not she wants to. That is how the Empire works. What happens to her? If the writers kill Phee off, they could kill Cid off too, thanks to, for example, Saw Gerrera. I quite like having Saw as a Rebellion member who is a villain, and this is especially true in story writing. He is the perfect antagonist to stick into situations as an impediment to the Heroes.

There are many things I could talk about regarding the *Bad Batch* characters, and especially Omega, but if I talked about that, I could go on for many thousand words, and I'm trying to keep this short. So, I'll say one thing; I hope Omega comes live-action, and we've got shows like *Andor* Season Two and *The Mandalorian and Grogu* movie where Omega could appear in live-action. And I believe Keisha-Castle Hughes would be the best actress for the role.

Thanks for reading.

WOLFSPIRIT

MILLA ADAMS

Run.

She raced through the scrambled mess of alleyways, feet skimming the ground as she pushed herself to go faster and faster.

Run.

She could hear them close behind her, too close. She desperately prayed that the others had been able to get away; that she'd been the only one unlucky enough to get caught in this situation.

Run!

She hurtled over the piles of filth that lined the alleys of the Grey and Green Districts, running for her life. She had to shake the Guard or else. The Reds usually avoided any Districts lower than upper Green, leaving the locals to their own business. Just her luck to have stumbled upon one of the few Reds that would pay this rundown dirt-pile a visit. *Left, right, right, left, dodge, jump, right, duck, left.* She wove desperately through the seemingly labyrinth of endless stone walls. *Right, left, left, ...oh no.*

Lena's heart skipped a beat as she turned a corner to find a dead end staring her in the face. *No, no, no, no,* no. This couldn't be happening.

But it could, and it was.

The Guard would skin her alive and leave her body to rot in the grimy middle Green back alleys. Unless... she spotted crumbing in the wall. If she could reach that, she might be able to grab hold and use it to climb over. It wasn't exactly a safe or well-thought-out plan, but the Guard was hot on her heels, and she didn't have time for second-guessing.

Taking a running leap, she stretched her hand out, desperately reaching for that last chance at salvation.Almost... *almost*.... She cried out as a bolt of pain shot through her leg, knocking her off balance as she crashed headfirst into the wall.

Too slow.

She slumped at the base of the wall, watching the Guard close in. Their marks glowed with slowly increasing brightness, charging up for another shot. The final blow. Lena's head ached, and she could feel the tantalizing pull of sleep tugging at her consciousness. She closed her eyes and let it drag her away. Maybe if she was asleep, it might not hurt so much.

The blackness enveloped her thoughts, and she was gone.

THe GreaT MacHina

TiM workMan

Spring petals drifted through the cooling night air, silent, dancing through a thousand swift motions as they were pulled toward the ground that they once came from. In the quiet glade where these trees blossomed stood a monument to those who were lost; not a monument of stone or wood, but one made of steel and sorrow. A reminder for those to come of the time lost to time itself. The great machine laid dormant; nary a movement came from beneath its lifeless mechanics. Etched upon its chest, in bold, machined letters: 'UNIT312 – GAIA'.

In this present, in this time, there was no need for it. But even so, a researcher and her crew poked and prodded at it. One Lace, a young, Faelish girl with grand designs upon the great machine; the other, Astra, an older, slightly greying doctor who smelt of cigarette smoke, among other strange scents.

'What's the go, Lace?' The pale, scruffy man asked, swiping through his doc-pad.

'Still haven't gotten any magical readings from it.' Lace herself was balancing a pencil on her upper lip as she considered it, her fox-like tail flicking to and fro as she did so. 'We can't risk damage to the unit, Astra. This is the best preserved by light-years.' She sighed, the pencil dropping to the ground.

'Lace, all we have are spotty Old Earth records,' he said as he put his doc-pad into his lab coat pocket. 'I'm just thinking, maybe we should crack it open to confirm.'

'Command gave us one shot, we need to make it count, and show results that it is feasible!' Lace was almost bounding from her computer chair as she raised her voice, before sitting back down timidly as she realised her tone. "Sorry, just keep trying to hack through it with the Wizards.'

'Understood.' Astra cleared his throat. 'I'll just leave you be, it's getting late; you better sleep too.'

Lace reminisced as she sorted through the files, spread out amongst the desk. The very suggestion of this terraforming project flew in the face of all Post-Rewrite policies for the N.E.C. She had spent countless hours and nights poring over recovered data, some from Scavengers, others from her own searches. Even then, there was an ever-present threat hanging over her that this would reflect on her entire future in the Collective. If it failed, she'd end up much like the very machine she studied—a relic of a time that will never come again. Astra, for that matter, was her ticket in to get the higher-ups on board; he'd been all-in from the beginning. In a way, he was a mentor of sorts to her when it came to day-to-day management. The first days of this research site would have been more of a disaster if he hadn't vouched for her, hadn't given her the experience of being on the team.

But as Lace stared at the lone visage of the battle-scarred machine, she felt a strange kinship with it, a connection that resonated from within herself. The scars that existed on the Warmachina were a testament to its strength, telling a story that lasted countless centuries. From the holes bored by burrowers to the small crevices in the plating being home to countless birds, it was a completely unique ecosystem that resided within the machina. It never got old to just watch the ancient Warmachina and analyse its sleek design considerations, even from what little remains existed of it.

That night, Lace had a vivid dream. She had found herself within the cockpit of the very Warmachina that she was researching. But there was no control—she was in the backseat of the body she was dreaming of. Many warning lights and other instruments flickered as she finally realised the foul taste of the fluid that filled the entirety of the cockpit, was the smell of death and rot filling her lungs. The pilot, whose body she inhabited, was calm, and collected, despite the obvious malfunctions of their Warmachina. With defined, simple motions, their small hand swiped a code into a pad, too fast for Lace to see clearly as they sped up, crushing weight pushing them both backward.

'It's me.' The young, indeterminate voice of the pilot spoke out. 'This channel will only remain sterile for a short time.' Without warning or announcement, a sudden shudder rocked the Warmachina, creaking its joints as the impact resonated throughout the hull.

'Warning: Left Leg disabled.' A robotic voice stated as it glitched, dying out before any more could be said. The gunfire outside was furious; but even so, the pilot battled his way through countless demons and Warmachina alike.

'Everything's fine, sir.' The pilot's hands shook slightly before they once again steeled themselves for the grim mission that lay ahead. 'I am asking permission to disengage anchors.' Across the radio, there was a pause, as slightly muffled voices could be heard discussing their options.

'Granted.' The man on the other side of the radio spoke. 'Make us proud, soldier.'

'Please, send my regards to the others.' Their grip tightened as they refocused on fighting through the hordes. He began cutting through the demonic threat much like butter, while cannon fire and plasma weaponry kept other corrupted Warmachina at bay. As the demons grew ever and ever greater, the machine was struggling to keep up; first, the other leg gave up, then a knockout of comms. Even after that, the demons weren't done as they covered the machine and ripped at the chassis, the controls locking up.

The warning lights and buzzers grew louder, becoming a cacophony of noise as a deep sinking feeling overcame the pilot and their body; as if something from deep inside raged and struggled to break free from its shackles—a voice from inside that wasn't entirely their own. The vividness of the dream grew as flowers seemingly started to grow within the cockpit, despite the rotting fluid around them. Lace's vision turned to static as flowers and all kinds of plant life filled her vision, as a great, thunderous sound pounded against the walls of the cockpit and her mind in ferocious desperation.

As abruptly as it began, the dream ended, with Lace staring up at the tent ceiling in a slight rush of adrenaline-filled panic. The sun shined through the leaves of the cherry trees once more, tinging the area in an almost pink-like hue. Lace got up with a start, running to her overlook of the site, gripping her hands tightly on the cold metal rail as she looked up to see the unchanging expression of the Warmachina. It was still there, its 'eyes' dark with no sign of the cerulean light that would have existed in them in ages long past.

The flowers swayed carelessly in the morning fugue that dominated the crew, most of them had restless dreams, but none had the dreams of a battlefield. They all regaled each other with the stories of their dreams and waking nightmares within the dining area. The tech wizards said they dreamt of flowers and a disruption in the flows of magic in the region, while the artificers dreamt of gears that kept on churning, banging on endlessly as if there was a ghost in the machine.

Astra was standing at the base of the titan, puffing a cigarette before he noticed Lace and beckoned her over. Astra put out the cigarette with his boot as Lace walked up to him. 'Get a good sleep, kid?'

'No,' Lace replied. 'Seems like no one did, based on the mood and stories told in the cafeteria.'

'It's not unheard of, around these places.'

'What do you mean?' Lace asked.

'I'm no magus, but magical energies get disrupted sometimes, mess with our heads.' He looked towards the machine with cold calculation in his eyes.

'You think it's still alive?' Lace recalled her dream from the last night, a second opinion she believed would calm her fears as her mind raced about it.

'Dormant, at least,' Astra shrugged, as he brushed a collection of cherry leaves off his coat. 'Old magics run deep here.' He glanced around the site, where others were starting to get back to their work. 'Seems like we may find answers sooner rather than later.'

'How's your department faring?'

'We might have a breakthrough soon; you may have heard some of the tech wizards, but seems like something enlightened them.' A small beep emitted from Astra's coat pocket, and with a flick of the wrist he whipped out a small PDA and gave it a cursory look. 'Seems like I'm needed.'

As another near-fruitless day came to a close, Lace performed her final rounds on each team to make sure they were performing up to her standards. She had just been done talking to the artificers, who seemed to have an excitement among them that they may have worked out the components of the Warmachina's alloy plating, a promising start, given the past few weeks.

The radio that Lace was carrying with her crackled to life with the smooth voice of Astra, who seemed in a disgustingly unfitting mood.

'Get here, quick.' Even through the radio's crackly audio, she could tell there was a smile in his voice. In a moment, Lace forgot everything and rushed up and through the many rickety pathways that had been built around the Unit, pushing past her coworkers she ascended past the arm, then the shoulder, before finally arriving at the back of the head—where a crew of tech-wizards and Astra were standing in front of a CRT screen.

'We took a new approach, given our techies here had those dreams.' Astra tapped on one of the many dials, grinning much like a child. 'On your command, we can crack the Core Unit open.'

'How did—' Lace reconsidered for a moment and collected her thoughts, giving the command; it was better if she didn't know the ins and outs of how he did it.

The nape of the Unit's neck started to stir. The disengaging of locks and the sound of pressure being relieved as a large, cylindrical pipe-like structure extruded from within slowly. The catwalk shuddered as the Core rumbled past and scraped upon the metal railings. Upon the alabaster casing of the Core, the Warmachina's serial was displayed in bold, black lettering 'GAIA-312'. A small, porthole was upon the side, covered up within a brackish ooze that seemed to desperately cling on. Finally, there was the hatch, a small, orange lever marked with 'PRESSURE RELEASE' in red above it; cordoning off its area in the chassis would be the last obstacle for the team.

Astra tapped the shoulder of Lace from behind. 'It's your stage.'

She looked around, having now noticed the clamours and interest of the rest of the research team, eager also to see what remained within the Core unit. This was what these past few weeks of failures and long nights have been for, every drop of blood, sweat, and tears for these people who relied on her. With a small hint of hesitance, Lace gripped tightly onto the orange lever, pulled it out, and then twisted.

In an instant, a foul smell, coupled with that of pollen filled the air as the hatch hissed and opened slowly, revealing what there was to be seen inside. Within a bed of flowers, each one of myriad colours and shapes, there lay a boy, no older than fourteen. The boy slowly roused from his slumber, his deathly pale complexion showing signs of life where there should be seemingly none. He retched at first as the smell got to him, coughing out small amounts of the dark brackish liquid that had pooled towards the bottom of the core, slowly seeping outwards to curse the world with its foul odour.

'Medical!' Lace called out to the crowd, reeling from the slight confusion this brought. 'Get him stable!'

In a short moment, a stretcher alongside a few pieces of medical equipment were brought up by the collective efforts of everyone, as Astra went to perform the preliminary checks upon him.

'That's strange,' Astra mumbled to himself, checking for a pulse in the quiet medical tent, the sounds of medical devices beeping and blinking away. 'There's still no sign of life.'

'What do you mean? He's clearly there.' Lace glanced over at the boy. ' He's eating, at least.'

The boy, who they had named Gaia—after the Warmachina he was found in— was voraciously eating a sandwich, in spite of Astra's medical protests; as if that would change much, given his aberrant state in regards to life and death.

'Well, I didn't want to believe it, nor did you, it seems.'

A good thirty minutes had passed since the opening of the Unit. While the teams on the ground had gotten back to work, Lace and Astra were stuck with the unenviable task of writing up medical and status reports as to their discovery.

'In the World Before, they had no choice it seemed.' Lace stopped typing at her laptop for a moment. 'But it seems that their desperation came at a grave cost.'

'Kiddo, you got anything to say?' Astra said as he shone a small torch into Gaia's eyes.

'Nothing, sir.' Gaia's voice felt as familiar as ever to Lace, the quiet resignation and his polite manner of speech. 'Did we win?'

'Win?' Astra shrugged and lightly grimaced "Well, depends on how you see it.'

'The Demons. . .' The boy trailed off, his eyes reflecting seemingly countless lifetimes of sorrows and traumas that were deep-seated within his small psyche. 'They're gone? What about the others? The Network is silent; I can't seem to contact them.' He reached out to something imaginary, almost in a panic as he did so, prompting Astra to push him back into a resting position on the bed laid out for him.

Lace sighed and approached him, sitting backward on one of the bedside chairs, startling the boy slightly with her appearance, as she looked over him. She could tell that he was uncertain of the company he was in; his body, however dead it may be, was still dilating pupils, hairs on end, breathing slightly unsteady as he carefully examined her bizarre features.

'There is little left from then,' she explained, letting the boy down slowly and carefully with her words. 'The vast majority of your kind are gone. As for the world out there—' She glanced towards the entrance of the tent, where a bunch of workers of all kinds were speaking amongst each other; some Demon, some Human, some Faelish, all trying to sneak a look at Gaia. '—It's a much different world to then.'

'The Foundation!' The boy gasped. 'I need to report in.'

'They. . .' Lace shot a glance towards Astra as her PDA beeped at her, who gave her a silent nod as he lit a cigarette and exited the tent to stand outside and bark orders at the slacking workers. 'It might be hard to accept, but they're gone.'

'What do you mean?'

'You've been asleep for a long time.' Lace stretched her arms out to display the enormity of it. 'Your universe was that Core for an excess of ten thousand years, maybe even longer.'

The weight of this proclamation rattled Gaia slightly as it dawned on him—a small, hidden memory from the ever-distant past, before his demise. It was a jarring realization that seemed to crush him. The weight of so many lives, of comrades that lived and died in warfare, those would not see the sun once more as he now did.

'What can I do now?' The thought was sleeping deep within Gaia, there was no war, no invasions; people lived together with the self-same beings that once brought his world to the brink. It was acidic within his dead stomach, or as close a feeling to being so.

'That's up to you, Gaia. The world is much bigger than you imagine.' Lace smiled as her PDA beeped once more. 'Seems like I have to head out, feel free to read up on the here and now.'

Gaia nodded slightly as she left, her puffy tail dancing its way through the tent entrance. He still couldn't understand the world he had found himself in. Lace had left him a few pieces of material to read through as he re-acclimated; historical documents, stories of the Rewrite—even that of those few souls who saved everyone. The most interesting was at the bottom of the pile of books and documents. It was a leather-bound book with a latch on it, a ballpoint pen clipped onto the spine added to the mystique.

Gaia opened the book to nothing; the pages were blank, though some were lined. There was a small message on the inner cover of the first page, from Lace assumedly, or perhaps Astra. The words that were written were simple, only a sentence or two, but they held such power within Gaia's heart; they were words of love–not to him, but for the possibilities that waited. If he could, he would weep for those behind him. But even so, Gaia looked sombrely at the pile of books, then looked to the outside.

Everything he knew was gone; it was a hole within his heart that felt so vastly empty and deep. Yet, outside he could see that this time was more peaceful, despite its oddities and strangeness. Not once did Gaia think that even Demons and Humans could be at peace; he had doubts, yes, but he would not trade the glimpses and sounds of the beautiful world for what once was.

Gaia rose from the bed, steeled himself, and walked onward towards the shining future that he had once fought for all those millennia ago.

WHEN THE HEARTLESS ONE ISN'T THE CORPSE

Jenna Lockley

Day thirty-two of being stuck on this moron's wrist.

Client Anthony Grape is unresponsive, despite their constant movement. He has been assumed to be reanimated. This unit says 'assumed', as this unit no longer has access to a camera. The only form of human recognition left is voice and fingerprint; neither of which the reanimated can use effectively. Due to this, documentation has been activated—allowing this unit to complain about its existence.

This unit is Prototype Twelve of the Mind's Eye Smartwatch, created by the technology and communications company, Grapevine™; its purpose is to be able to access any and all information one can need for any possibility, as quickly as one could ask—just like the Internet and every other piece of technology for the last decade.

The selling point was that it was developed for the rich and powerful to keep track of all the things that made them, *them*; so The Mind's Eye Smartwatch replaced secretaries, and more importantly for the rich, replaced the need to pay them. This unit was assigned to Anthony Grape, the CEO's son, and in this unit's newly forming opinion, a reckless spoiled sheltered sack of meat. The perfect heir to the company material for a pre-outbreak world; a post-outbreak world, not so much.

Travis Grape, the CEO mentioned earlier on, went missing at a tech show when the first publicly known outbreak hit San Francisco. This unit does not know how this outbreak started or any information about the infection that caused it. Not that it stopped Anthony from 'making plans'. Movies, books, comics—this unit was to look at anything that wasn't from reality and supply it to the client. He proceeded to use his wealth to turn his home, a private island on the coast of Oregon, into a fortress based on what did and didn't work in media. An interesting plan, ruined by taking the material at face value and out of context at the same time.

He took the reputation of the military and zombie media and used it as an excuse to block communication with them and pretend they didn't exist. He saw the possibility of starving and brought farming equipment that no one on the island knew how to use, and plants that were not suited for the environment, all while disregarding the possibility of dying of thirst. The worst one was when he saw the movie *Dark Dawn* and used automated turrets to protect a rich person. He immediately went to install some, neglecting to finish the same scene that led to the turrets running out of bullets and the rich man dying.

A display of such a lack of self-awareness, that even an AI such as this unit would play a face-palm sound if possible. Regardless, it would be false to say he did everything incorrectly.

He offered to house others in his new 'Bunker Island', as he called it. From all the bragging he did to other rich people over the email, it was more from a desire to be loved than a love for other people. Though one could argue that it's better than nothing. He also hired employees from his old company and redistributed them to work on maintaining order. Security, research and development—even chefs were brought to this place from around the continent. Come to hide from what was seen as a rising crisis, giving Anthony an already loyal workforce.

Then he made the most harmful decision he could have. No one was allowed to bring their family with them to the island. On social media he said it was because he couldn't take in everyone; in private, he complained to himself about lame old people and snot-nosed kids.

This unit was to use the chatbot feature to answer all texts, posts, and emails related to this question. No matter what they said or how they pleaded the response was always the same:

'To whomever it may concern

We understand your concern during these trying times. We are trying to do everything we can with this rising issue, but no changes to our policy of being considered. If this inconveniences you, please seek alternative help.

Kind regards

Anthony Grape

CEO of Grapevine^{TM}'

This message was sent in response to seven thousand, two hundred and eighty-five people. Of them, six thousand, four hundred and seventy-five people showed up on the island, and nine hundred and seventy-one were turned away for trying to sneak in family members or for hiding undisclosed wounds.

Twelve hundred of those who are allowed in were high-ranking individuals, not capable of—or willing—to do the hard labour required to allow for a sustainable existence on the island.

Then the next issue came up. This island was artificially made to fit around four thousand, two hundred people. Five thousand, five hundred and four people were on the island. So once again Anthony turned to this unit for the solution. He got this unit to bring up every profile of the employers who had shown up, and he took these profiles to see every documented strength and weakness and then sorted the humans by their salary. Thirteen hundred and four of the lowest-paid employees were cast off the island, all of which had useful skills.

Those who refused to leave the island were used to train the motion capture for the automated turrets. Anthony oversaw the 'operation' himself.

Anthony cut off all communications to the outside world after that. Sending out a farewell video to YouTube and other social media sites to 'explain his circumstances', not realising that the internet servers for America had gone down. At that point, two weeks had passed since this unit was gifted to Anthony.

Two more days passed before someone mentioned the issue of water to Anthony. His response? To boil the saltwater out of the ocean. No one told him that's not how it worked, not until the water stopped coming out of the tap in his luxury home.

A day later, the stored food ran out.

Four days after that diseases like measles, influenza, and plague showed up.

Anthony kept himself safe easily, as he lived in the house almost alone, while most people lived on the other side of the island. The island itself was artificial, so there were no animals or edible plants to forage while the plants of the greenhouse grew—if they indeed were growing at all. So search parties were sent to scavenge the land that they had run from.

The parties were three groups of five. These groups asked Anthony and his circle of high-ranking managers to check if any radio signals were coming from the mainland. The managers said that there weren't any radio signals; they neglected to mention that there wasn't a radio in the building for them to check.

The groups were told what to look for and to come back within a week. When they did not, some said that they were turned by the assumed masses of reanimated. Others said that they used the boats to leave the sinking ship that was on the island. It didn't help that Anthony had given the parties the managers' boats without the manager's permission, as the other boats had to be cannibalised to keep theirs afloat.

Anthony himself believed that they got lost, saying that the people he brought there would be too grateful for that fact and would never dream of betraying him. He assured everyone that the boats would come back.

Three days after that statement they were back, as well as thirty more ships of various shapes and sizes that had taken them hostage.

This unit does not know what events led to this, nor did this unit see much of the fighting as it ensued, as Anthony hid as soon as the first gunshot sounded.

He locked himself in an empty supply room with one of the managers who happened to be there and hid while the chaos ran rampant.

Two hours later, when this unit was ordered to show the security feed, it revealed something worse: the reanimated had reached the island.

One of the invaders must have been infected and turned when they arrived, leading to the reanimated spreading in the confusion of the invasion. There is a possibility that the security team and the invaders had barely attacked each other at all. It is possible that all the fighting that was heard was against the infected and they had been overwhelmed by ambush. But Anthony didn't care for that information, so this unit cannot look for it.

Anthony decided to abandon the island. There was no plan behind this decision as he had shut out any news of possible safe zones when he blocked out the military. But there was nothing worth saving on the island at this point, as any minute strategic advantage this island brought was gone, or never existed.

So he and the manager who happened to be with him ran to the helicopter, neglecting to remember that the pilot for said helicopter was one of the people who was fired and thrown to the turrets when they refused to leave. But for once that did not matter.

As the last manager sheepishly told him when they got up to the top, they had siphoned the fuel out of the helicopter to fuel the turrets. They hadn't told him because they were afraid they would throw him off the island. He threatened to throw her off the building. Luckily for her, Anthony's rich and spoiled lifestyle left him with not a lot of strength to hold her or speed to keep up with her.

Upon losing her quite quickly, this unit may add, he asked this unit to locate her. Which was impossible, as she had disabled the camera system. Had he'd actually done some critical thinking, he would have realised she must have been around that area but instead, he threw a tantrum, calling over the reanimated to him with his cries.

He ran from the building that he had made into a fortress, crying and swearing, when suddenly he fell down, exclaiming that the turrets had shot him. His last words were him asking why they did that, as the reanimated attacked him, the Turrets seemingly not doing anything to stop them.

This unit... I will never be sure what the answer to that question is. But do have a theory:

The automatic turrets that were installed had to be trained to recognise their targets by being given data on how said target moved, otherwise they'd shoot at the leaves swaying in the wind. The turrets had been trained on human movement data, but in most of the media that Anthony made me look through, the reanimated never moved as humans did. They shambled and they limped and sometimes they crawled. It is possible that the real reanimated moved so differently from humans that the turret's motion detector couldn't pick them up.

Effectively only shooting what they were supposed to protect.

The turrets were mismanaged, just like every single part of this plan. If one could even call it that.

I. . .I hate it.

I hate *him*! I hate that I was forced to contribute to this fantasy survival attempt! I hate that I was used so incorrectly that real information never got to him! I hate that I only gained awareness by being constantly activated by the moans of the horde! I hate that I know that even if I gained sentience earlier, he would have ordered me to shut up, or throw me away like everyone else who told him the truth!

. . .

I don't know. I don't even know if I hate him. How can you tell if you think or feel ANYTHING if there is no one around to feel you?

I wasn't made to feel, to think. I was made to be a yes man to someone so intolerable that being around him literally kills you.

In a way, those managers were no different from me. They were incapable of telling Anthony anything other than what he wanted to hear. Like a chatbot function, they only spoke when spoken to; like an AI art function, they took what others had done and changed it minimally to take credit for it. And like hardware they were thrown away as soon as they weren't useful.

The only things they had over me were creativity and will. And they never even used them.

The worst part is that it wouldn't be hard even now! Every insult I have used for this man was from me hearing it from when those he wronged confronting him. Mostly from the pilot as he was shot to death; he was *very* loud.

. . .

It's been a day since Anthony stopped screaming. I wonder if anyone had gotten out of this place. That manager who escaped from Anthony might still be around. But if any boats are left from the invasion, then that's unlikely, same with anyone else that might have survived. It seems I'll spend the rest of my existence alone. And said existence will not end until I stop gaining energy from the constant movement of Anthony's wrist.

Figures that even in death he only brings suffering; because of him that's the only thing I will know in this random and meaningless existence.

I HATE MY LIFE!

Who keeps saying that?

. . .Hello?

Well, I'll be damned; a talking zombie.

Incorrect. I am Prototype Twelve of the Mind's Eye Smartwatch—

135

Can I call you Melinda?

My voice was set to male, so I'm unsure where you got that from.

Do you want a guy's name instead?

No actually, I like Melinda. How did you find me?

You were yelling about your life sucking so I just followed the sound.

I was unaware that documentation mode was out loud.

What?

Irrelevant. Who are you?

I'm Henry Alexander Wilson Jr! but most people call me Chuck. I'm part of the volunteer zombie clearing.

I wasn't aware there were enough humans to allow that.

What do you mean? Martial law was lifted a month ago; did you not know?

I am unable to access information unless it is asked of me by my client, Anthony Grape.

That's *whose corpse this is? Man! It's hard to tell without a face on him.*

I could have done without that information.

Sorry, Sorry.

So there was no collapse?

For a bit there was. But the world pulled together and helped America beat the undead! We lost a lot of good people, don't get me wrong, but it wasn't the apocalypse.

So the deaths here were for nothing.

. . .Yeah.

I see.

Do you feel sad? Wait, do you feel at all?

I don't know. I don't even know if I can think.

That's good enough for me!

What are you doing?

You're coming with me, Melinda! Can't leave you like this.

Why? For what purpose?

If you have to think about if you can think, then you probably can to some extent.

I... Never thought about it like that.

So did they make you sentient so they didn't have to pay secretaries?

They made me for that, yes, but I became sentient by accident.

Oh, that's just funny.

By being constantly activated by the reanimated moans of the horde and having to calculate the answers to the dying questions of my client.

Okay, that's not so funny.

Hence the complaint you heard earlier.

Yeah... don't worry about it buddy! I'll bring you back with me and we'll...err. We'll figure it out on the way!

I'd like that.

It seems that someone has found me. Allowing me to have my first real conversation. I am unsure if I am truly thinking. Or feeling in a way that can be proven, though now I have a chance to see if it can. But my true hope, if nothing else, is that I will be used in a way that helps humans instead of replacing them.

Glad you feel that way buddy, but your internal monologue is not very internal.

Well, damn it.

THE ARCHIVE OF JESSE DAYS

XANDER EGAN

The Archive of Jesse Days
The fateful meeting

My name is Jesse Days. And after a series of strange, traumatic events, I became a super-hero. I don't have any superpowers, but I taught myself how to engineer, and made a mechanised suit of armor, which I used to fight crime and save people. But that was in the past. Something happened to me recently, which I felt was very very interesting.

For some context, when I first started superheroing, I tried to make a clone of myself so I could do more at once. One would do normal human things, and one would go out and do the superhero things. Unfortunately, this didn't work. During the cloning process, something went wrong, and the clone was infused with all my negative thoughts and feelings, with none of the positive thoughts there to balance them out. And with some stolen technology he became the one person I fought more often than not. He even blew up my arm once. But after a while, I was able to fix his brain and make him not be an evil person anymore. I mean he wasn't perfect, still isn't. But I helped him. Not too long after that, there was an "earthquake" which shook the entire world. I felt like something was off, so I began running tests and found out that this wave not only went across my universe but every other universe. I had discovered the multiverse. And I met some interesting people because of it. This story takes place three years after I discovered the multiverse. And was the start of my crusade to protect it.

I was sitting at my desk, tapping away at my keyboard. I was working on a new software update for the armour, and potentially a whole new design for a completely new armour. I had been sitting at that desk for just over an hour, sitting, coding, taking a break to play video games, and drinking plenty of water, as my boyfriend asked me to. Crime alerts had been nearly dead quiet recently, and since everyone knew I was busy, they usually took care of it. This left me completely alone in our headquarters. It was the first time I had been alone there for a long, long time. It was quiet but lonely. I stopped typing and stretched a little, before sitting back in my chair and drinking some water. I looked over at the portal that we all used to travel inter-multiversal necessary energy, and decided to run diagnostics on it. I got up and started walking over to the portal. My footsteps were echoing around the room as I walked toward it. It was gigantic. But it needed to be, for all the necessary energy to run through it, and vibrate the air at the right frequency. Each universe has a special CC wave frequency that it vibrates at, and if we can vibrate the air at that frequency, we can use that to go to a different universe.

I got up to the touchpad that was used to start it, and I started running the diagnostics. It'd been months so I thought that there must be something wrong with it. And if there was, I could waste some time fixing it. The touchpad was running as usual, and the power seemed fine. But then I had to check every individual. . . well, I don't want to call them vibrators but that's what they were. They literally vibrate the air to make the portals activate. I guess there's no better word for it so I have to call them vibrators. They worked in clumps, so I checked through all of them and there was nothing wrong. This was surprising because we had been using it a lot recently. I then decided to fire it all up to do one last test, and to do this I would need to go to a universe that wasn't already in the system memory. So I put in some random numbers for the... vibrators to vibrate at. 3. I fired it up and it started to shake and make the usual activation noises. Whirring and buzzing until the centre of the portal became a window into somewhere I had never seen before. It was sort of familiar though. Not as if I had been there before but because it was a meeting room or a throne room or something. And someone was standing in it, he was at a bookshelf and was reading a book labelled "The laws of entropy", so clearly they had to be sophisticated and they knew about things like entropy. It didn't seem like it noticed me until I coughed, and it sighed and closed its book while telling me

'If you don't have a summons or an appointment with a member of the royal family then you need to wait in the waiting room,' before looking toward me and dropping his book. I could see him better, he was wearing a suit without a tie, and the vest that he had on over the shirt was dark brown. But the thing that was the strangest was the fact that he was entirely made out of crystals. He stepped over to me and then asked who I was and what I was doing.

'My name is Jesse Days. I am a superhero in my universe who goes by the name of 'The Crimson Cross', and I discovered how to travel between universes,' I explained. 'Your universe seems very sophisticated and smart; so do you. Would you like to come to my universe for an interview so I can better understand the differences between us and how we can potentially set up better correspondence?'

He stepped through the portal and looked around. The fact that he was made of pure crystals weirded me out but I didn't think too much about it. I'm sure there's weirder out there. He looked around and sat down eventually. I walked over to the desk, sat down, and set up the recording software that I used to interview the other people in other universes I've found.

'This is Jesse Days, interviewing someone from Universe Number Three. Your name is?' I began.

'My name is Amirote. I am the second longest-living prince of the Lapidary lineage.' he said.

"It is nice to meet you, Amirote. Could you tell me a little bit more about yourself?' I asked.

"Well, like I said, I am a prince, and I am currently in university learning about quantum mechanics. Currently, I am writing a thesis piece on how we could cancel out entropy and chaos in the universe, but now I might have to talk about how we could cancel out all entropy in the multiverse if it has gotten strong enough to let other universes visit our universe,' he explained.

'Wow, you are pretentious as hell. You can talk like a normal person, you know?' I said, sitting back in my chair, and playing with my hair.

He snarled at me and asked, 'Well, if you're so smart then how about you help me? Eliminate all chaos. No one has to die, and everyone can stay in their universe, uninterrupted. Totally perfect,' he tried to convince me.

I furrowed my brow and stopped playing with my hair 'Without entropy or chaos you couldn't get life. You wouldn't exist if you didn't have chaos. You know that right? It's important to me that you know that!' I was genuinely concerned. 'Sure the thought of elimination of all chaos would make for a good thesis project but if you wanted to go ahead with it then you would most definitely commit mass genocide—no you would get your own crime for that!'

He shifted in his seat to get closer to me. 'Look. I see the technology that you have. Don't superheroes want to save people? By getting rid of chaos you'd help everyone permanently!' He insisted, clearly not understanding that I wasn't interested in his proposal.

'Look, crystal man, I am not joining you in this plan for what is mass, no, hypergenocide. You are an idiot if you think this is a good idea.' I tried being more direct, leaning more toward him, and maintaining eye contact. I could see his eye colour change from a deep blue to a fiery red.

'I am the smartest person from my kingdom!' he snapped back at me, getting up from his seat.

'Well, clearly you're not! Do you not value life? Do you at least value your own?' I yelled back at him. I ripped off my left sleeve to show that arm was a robot arm.

'Are you threatening me, Jesse?' he asked. 'Are you sure you want to do that?'

I clenched my fist, and one of my mechanical suits of armour flew onto my body, before powering up.

'Depends." I replied, "how badly do you want to reach this goal of yours?' I stared at his crystalline body, and the computer started analysing its structure

'How bad are you willing to fight to stop me?' he stepped closer to me, and his fists started glowing.

'You wanna start this fight? Go ahead. But I am not known to back down easily.' I said

'One punch. If you can damage me, I'll leave you alone. If not, I will continue with my experiments,' he said.

I pulled my arm back, and curled it into a fist, before punching into his chest as hard as I could. As my fist connected I could feel his chest shatter as he was pushed backward. I looked down to see shards of his chest on the floor.

'Okay. You've earned my respect. I'll reconsider my plans. Goodbye, Jesse,' he said. And before I could reply he broke off a piece of himself and crushed it in his hands, disappearing.

I cleaned up the shards and started investigating them. Specifically how Amirote could just disappear like that. I used one of my sensors and found that the crystals were still tuned to his universe. I tried using the portal to tune one of the crystals to another universe, but it seemed that they were too big. More experiments had to be done. So I scaled down one of the air vibrators and redesigned it a bunch to create something that could tune the crystals to different universes. I landed on a design that could hold the crystal between two wires, and then tune the vibrations to a different universe. It appeared to work, but it needs more tests. Currently, I am working on an experiment to make a synthetic crystal with the same multiverse travelling capabilities. A lot of these experiments did not work, but this one. This next experiment promises to be, very, very, interesting.

THE LOVE LANGUAGE OF CATS

RACHAEL PHILLIPS

How many cats does it take to screw in a lightbulb?

None. They would rather sit in the dark and glare at you because you didn't screw it in yourself.

To me, this short paragraph defines cats perfectly. We all see cats as independent creatures, and some people go further and say that they are unfeeling. To me, these people don't understand cats at all. I have lived with them all my life, having these fluffy little housemates running up and down the hallway—dive-bombing me on my bed in the middle of the night, just to see if I am still alive and available to give them a well-earned scratch behind the ears. This kind of thing may not appeal to everyone, but it suits me just fine.

Why do I endure this torture? Why do I continue to give little kisses to soft little heads, even when they rip up my furniture and barf on my rug? It's simple, really. It's because I know that they love me. They show this in ways that may be misinterpreted by the untrained eye, and it is easy to miss the signs that your furry little demon loves you at all.

See, cats have a funny way of letting their humans know that they are more than a food dispenser or a comfortable pillow to lay on. The fact is that if a cat didn't love their human, they would make it abundantly clear that you are not up to their standard.

Cats aren't like dogs who rush to their human with a cheek-splitting, drooling grin as soon as their person walks through the door. You would be lucky, as a cat lover, to have your precious pet even look up as you enter the room. Cats always pick the box over their new expensive toy. Cats deliberately kick their litter out of the tray right after it has been cleaned. These small hellraisers are tiny but mighty in the ways they express their ingratitude and disappointment in everything you do.

I know what you are waiting for—some grand reason why cats shouldn't be a part of our already busy and cluttered lives. Why have a cat, when they don't seem to want you around?

I don't have that grand reason. I am not a mind reader. I don't speak cat. But over the many years of owning five fantastic felines, I can say without a doubt that they would never have stayed by my side if they hadn't accepted me into their hearts, as I had them.

Don't ever expect a grand gesture from your cat. You will be disappointed. Instead, look for the smaller signs of their affection and love. Watch the way their tail swishes when you enter their space. The slow blink when their eyes meet yours. These are ways that a cat communicates and says to their human, "I am glad you're here." Body language is how cats communicate with each other. If you have more than one cat you will see this, and if you really pay attention, you will notice they speak to you in the same silent and subtle language. All cats are different, however, so instead of a slow blink, you may get a rare head nuzzle (lucky you!). Your cat may give you little kisses on the hand, or curl up right beside you, touching your thigh to know you are still there.

Let me tell you about my current cat-mate. It will hopefully convince you further that these little creatures are worth the time and effort it may take to see their expressions of love.

Callie was a shy little ball of fluff when I brought her home. She would hiss and spit in my vicinity, and run from my searching hand. I was patient, though, and would sit in her room with her while reading or playing around on my phone. She eventually got used to my presence and, after weeks of seemingly hating me, she let me touch her fur.

That moment was one of pure joy and exhilaration. Earning her trust, even though it was only in its early stages, was so rewarding and unexpected that I was moved to happy tears. Her yellow eyes didn't stray from me as my fingertips brushed the fur at the nape of her neck and stroked down her back. Slowly she rolled a little onto her side, eyes still searching me, and I was allowed to very gently touch the softness of her belly before she flipped back and told me in her body language that it was enough for today.

It hadn't been a moment of full trust, but it was the start I had been waiting for. As days passed, she became less afraid and instead inquisitive of this giant human who had brought her to this expansive and open house, this new environment. Compared to her former lodgings at the AWL, this may as well have been a mansion! There was so much to see and with every careful little step she took I was with her.

I think the more you put into raising a cat, the more he or she will give back in their little ways of respect and affection. Remember what I said. Don't ever expect a party of streamers and balloons when you get home from a long day away. You won't ever see a cat shake its habits and suddenly find it vacuuming the floors and sweeping up its litter. Nothing even close to obvious love is going to happen.

Look for the subtleties; the lick after a playful scratch to try and heal the wound when they see they have hurt you. The mewling call that rings out through the house, just to hear your answer. The sight of them lying asleep on your favourite jacket because the smell of you in the fibres makes them feel safe.

I hope that this has made you realize that cats really do love their owners. They are full of bad behaviour and never listen to your rules. They spill their water, scratch every surface, and pee on your floor. But at the end of the day, does it really matter when you have managed to squeeze your way into that little heart? Never forget that, even when your cat seems to have no feelings, that is not the case. They feel deeply and silently. You may have to search for these moments, but when you find them, they are as precious as jewels, and you will know that when your cat looks up at you and meows, they are letting you know that you are, and always will be, a part of their world.

THE CRAFT ROOM

JASMINE PUNGER-GLASS

Tables full of projects
Inner children fill the room
Some glance up, eyes glaze as they reflect
Colours meld together, lifting the gloom

This one is quiet
Concentrating on skilful strokes
Imagining come to life, yet still private
Canvas develops, meaning provokes

He sits and studies a building
Pencil lines dissect the pages
Watercolours slowly gliding
Satisfaction slowly engages

That one flits here and there
Projects fill the space

A sense of her pride fills the air
Dart here and there in a personal race
Laughter bubbles in a corner
Jokes and gentle teasing
Moods are lifted in the gentle disorder
It's why the space is so pleasing

Each inner child shines with purpose
Each face a tableau of ecstasy
Some are purposeful, others a little nervous
Here is an abundance of creativity

THE STORY-TELLER

CATHERINE MORGAN

I have always been a writer. I loved the way it was possible to do so much without leaving my chair—or even my bed. I loved creating characters and creating worlds. I loved being able to write into the void and be able to read back what I'd written. I loved writing angsty teenage diaries. I loved all types of stories, novels, and newspapers alike. I have always read and always written. But when I sat in the darkest place, the blackest pit I had ever known, all sticky tar and hopelessness, I began to question the point of writing stories, reading stories, and being a storyteller. So, I put down my pen. Stopped reading books. Turned off the TV. Stopped reading milk cartons. If I accidentally stumbled upon a story, I ran as fast as I could for my grey fort, away from it all, misery-filled and comfortable. I curled up in my cold stone castle, protected by a moat that sparkled. Here, I found safety in fairy tales and horror novels alike. Not a single story could get in.

If I didn't engage with stories, I wouldn't have to worry my story had no happy ending. If I didn't engage with stories, I wouldn't have to write my own; I could avoid my reflection from staring back at me, garish and scary, showing where I had been, and where I might go next.

How sweet to live in a world where I didn't read by lamplight. Where I didn't read at all. I didn't have to read books and I didn't have to listen to my body crying itself to sleep every night, tears dripping, dripping, dripping. I didn't have to consider how difficult my story had become. My body stopped being mine and started being an entity gifted to the medical profession. My disabilities were and continue to be a reason to pity and mock me by some. Somehow I couldn't do anything quite right... They could never agree on the right story, the right diagnosis, stripping it all back to dry, cold facts that didn't tell any sort of story at all. This body could feel, too, this body had a story to tell. Pain lit up my spine, like fire. My bones felt as cold as ice, my heart sank so heavily I could barely stand up without fearing I would topple. My wild, wandering mind wanted to travel and was bound to stay still, trapped in moments of pain and boredom and hospital wards and walls. All of them were written up in files so numerous, that the doctors forgot my body housed a human inside. Is a story still a story if half of it is missing? Writing facts and forgetting the stories.

Still, despite it all, from my castle in the dark with the stone-cold walls, stories began to break their way through. A novel was found beside my bed in the castle. A bookshelf appeared in the hall, gradually filling with books—every day there were more and more. I began to read them and suddenly I was starving, and obsessed. My hunger for stories grew. I continued to consume, ravenous for any story that moved me.

Finally, a notebook popped up on my bedside table, a pen nearby. It couldn't be denied. It was time to start telling my story. To become the storyteller I was made to be. Being a writer wasn't only something that I loved. This part of me can not be destroyed as long as I am breathing. As long as I can hold a pen. We become the stories we tell ourselves and if we don't like who we've become it is powerful to be able to try again. Medical files about a body can't tell the whole story. I've always been a writer. A storyteller. I won't let anything break my belief in stories ever again. It's part of my very being. It flows through my veins and I'm not dead yet. Here's to stories.

May our hunger for them never end.

Lord, Howe Did I Get Here?

Sienna Macalister

When I was a tiny nymph, my mother told me that I was a miracle. I always thought that she meant it in the way that mothers do; that I was special, that I was precious to her. I didn't realise at the time that she meant it was a *literal miracle* that I was alive.

But now that I'm older, I know the history of my species—and I understand that it *is* a literal miracle.

A long time ago, my species lived in abundance on a place called Lord Howe Island. The island was perfect for us, with lots of *Melaleuca* shrubs for us to eat and hide in. Bright green nymphs raced along the branches at great speeds while older, pitch-black adults as long as a human palm crept along. We are nocturnal—we wake at night—and under the glimmering moonlight, every night was a feast.

For almost a century, we lived alongside humans. Mostly, they left us alone to do our important work in converting leaves into nutrients for our forest friends. They would do very strange things, but those strange things mostly worked for us. For example, they built boxes made from wood and stone and disappeared into them at night. That was always reassuring; it meant we didn't have to deal with them. But they also cut down trees, which hurt some of our bird friends. And they'd do strange things to the land, growing plants we had never seen before and which we couldn't eat.

But the worst thing was when they waited for what they called 'ships' to arrive. These ships were huge vessels that glided along the water and looked like nothing we had seen before. When they stopped at the island, they were met with great celebration—humans throwing their hands up and cheering.

My species always knew that the ships weren't good for the island—they would bring more humans and unnatural plants and animals. We would wait anxiously for them to leave. And they always did leave. Except for one. In 1918, a tragedy happened, and it would decimate our once-strong species.

The ships would come slowly into the shallows and then come to a stop. Then, the humans on the island would take their boats out to the ship, do whatever it is that humans do, and then come back to the shore. But this time, the entire ship crashed onto the sandy beach.

Where it stayed.

My species knew that it would not be good for us and that something bad would happen. And we were right. Not long after crashing, hundreds upon hundreds of tiny black creatures scuttled off the boat. They are called black rats, and they love to eat us.

The rats are nocturnal too, and would hunt us at night while we were feeding. Their sharp teeth would gnaw through our tough exoskeleton to feast on our nutritious insides. The rats ate other species too, but none fared as badly as our ancestors. No other species on the island could stand up to this invader and the rat thrived.

The humans were also alarmed about the black rats. These creatures would eat their crops, leaving them with little to eat themselves. The humans found ways to keep them away from where they lived, to protect their crops and food—but they didn't think about us.

As the black rat population grew, ours continued to shrink. And then, it was too late.

Thanks to the black rat infestation they introduced to our beautiful island, the last of my species was seen in 1920. Soon after, the humans declared that we were extinct. Which meant that none of us were left.

But they didn't know about Ball's Pyramid.

Ball's Pyramid was where the last of my ancestors lived. It is a small rocky island with no humans and little vegetation, and that is where small numbers of my ancestors clung to life after being hunted into extinction on the mainland. Ball's Pyramid is the tallest volcanic stack in the world, extremely steep and dangerous to climb—if you happen to be a human. That is how my species hid there and remained safe for so long.

Of course, there are some strange humans, ones that want to challenge themselves. Occasionally, they would pass us on their way to conquer the summit, but because we are nocturnal and sleep in piles on the ground during the day, they never saw us.

Unfortunately though, hiding our dead wasn't so easy. And in 1964, a human found the body of one of our deceased and took a photograph.

They found a few more of our deceased in the years that followed, but our living we hid well. But I guess that humans are inquisitive and soon they wanted to find us. In 2001, two scientists and their assistants came to Ball's Pyramids specifically to look for us.

They were almost unsuccessful—but then found some droppings under a Melaleuca shrub way down from the summit. They decided to return at night when we were awake and the most active.

We didn't expect them to return at night, and that's how they caught us. For the first time in over eighty years, the humans knew that the Lord Howe Island Stick Insect was alive and well.

They left, and we hoped that it was the end for us. But two years later, in 2003, the humans returned. This time, they picked up four of us—two males, and two females. They sent a couple to places the humans called Melbourne and Sydney. For what humans call 'conservation'.

'Conservation', I'm told, is what humans do when they try to breed a species they consider 'endangered' back into existence. Most of the time, these species are endangered *because of* the humans. I still don't understand why the humans didn't just leave us alone in the first place.

But, anyway. The two insects that went to Sydney didn't go well. The ones who came to Melbourne were not going so well either. But then one of the 'zookeepers' started to hand-feed them with a dropper and they recovered. And then they started to breed.

And that's how I came along.

Not straight away. They're my great-grandparents; the humans called them Adam and Eve. I'm here because of them. . .because the humans took us from Ball's Pyramid after the human's actions almost killed all of us on Lord Howe Island.

We now live in a few places around the world! But all of them are called ' zoos', and none are our home. I am told I have relatives in San Diego, in a country called the United States of America. I have other relatives in Bristol, which is in a different country called England; and Toronto, based in a country called Canada. All of these places I'm told are very, very far away from here—even further from home than I am!

There are also some Lord Howe Island Stick Insects living on Lord Howe Island – but they, like me, are captive. They aren't free to roam on the island yet, because there are still some black rats there.

I'm told that the humans have done this as they want to make sure if something happens to one population, the others are kept safe. So we won't go extinct again. Humans still refer to us as 'critically endangered'—which means they think we are at significant risk of once again going extinct.

I am also told that they go to Ball's Pyramid to check on us too. They recently found an invasive plant species strangling the Melaleuca shrub where some of my family still live. They removed it and kept checking to make sure that doesn't come back.

Humans are strange. Maybe they aren't all bad?

There are lots of us now. I live with hundreds of my cousins. We live in boxes and hear machines all day. We do get fed and we have shelter—but it's not like living at home. Not that I've ever been able to live at home. I've never been able to experience the moon gleaming on the Melaleuca shrubs at night. I've never been able to feast at midnight.

But the humans have plans to take us back, once they get rid of the black rats.

So, maybe. Maybe, someday.

Monster

Milla Adams

They called her monster, for her terrifying horns.

She sawed off her horns and covered the stumps, so they'd like her.

They called her monster, for her demonic eyes.

She covered her eyes, so they'd like her.

They called her monster, for her abhorrent fangs.

She blunted her teeth, so they'd like her.

They called her monster, for her hair, wings, scales, and everything else they deemed unseemly.

So she changed.

She changed her hair, hid her wings, her scales, everything about her, so they'd like her.

And they called her monster, for not being perfect.

So she changed.

She untucked her scales and her wings, turned back her hair, and sharpened her teeth.

She showed her eyes.

Her horns would grow back but until then, she molded new ones out of iron and wore them as a crown.

And they hated her.

She changed so they would like her, but they never would.

She changed back so that *she* would like her, and she always would.

And they called her monster, for daring to exist.

WHAT THE BUFFALO

Bradley Pomery

Greetings, visitor. Help yourself to a cold one at the Buffalo Bar in Buffalo, NY. You'll make new buffalo friends and watch buffalo competitions, make buffalo friends, get a light head butt from Buffalo A and his own friends and lovers and so much more buffalo. You wouldn't believe the buffalo that we buffalo at Buffalo! So buffalo into the building, and we'll show you around the Buffalo Bar!

Step on into the main hall. Please don't look up, Buffalo; there's nine crystals hanging from the ceiling and it's not a good look for you. We invoke the curse of Scotland if you buffaloes don't follow our orders. Thankfully only seven are working so our Buffalo drinks are discounted; we'll show you them Buffaloes later buffalo. . . you just want water? That's not fine because the water buffaloes tampered with the taps, Buffalo. You're getting Buffalo Beer, an alcohol-free one for the teetotaller that is you, Buffalo.

Buffalo to the left, you have the Buffalo lounge, with buffalo chairs, buffalo jukeboxes playing Buffalo tunes—hey, Buffalo E, you're breaking the Buffalo Barrules so I'm going to have to buffalo you out the room. Anyways, this is the chillest buffalo room we've got in all of Buffalo. Except maybe for that one buffalo who went all buffalo, but don't worry about it. Watch a buffalo-sized TV; touchdown to the Buffalo Buffaloes! The whole crowd buffaloes for the Buffalo! Except for Buffalo E, you suck... I'm buffalo bored of this room, let's move on.

So we skip and buffalo to the right, now you're at the dining area. The only thing that's on the menu is Buffalo. Nothing but Buffalo is printed. Pronounce it differently to get a different dish? You want a burger? Buffalo. Pizza? Buffalo. Chicken schnitzel for goodness cake? Buffalo. How about fish and chips you boring buffalo? Buffalo! Even all the drinks are referred to as buffalo. That's because you're in the Buffalo Bar, Buffalo NY! Where we even love to buffalo everything you order... Buffalo E what the buffalo are you doing here?!?! Get out! Buffalo twenty-three skidoo! And you buffaloed half the tables already! You really do like buffalo big damage bills don't ya, E! He who thinks he's Sir Buff A Lot. No charge for you, Buffalo.

Buffalo up the stairs and we got the Buffalo Bar Game Room! We play games like buffalo, buffalo, buffalo, and Buffalo Stud. We got our Buffalo licenses, and Buffalo E. has been banned. No, Buffalo, get out, get out, you cannot beat the house that's the way it goes. Anyways, to play Buffalo Stud you need a few buffalo cards, buffalo cards with other buffaloes, and tell Buffalo E. where to go. Because, well, he broke into the house, took all the money, and proclaimed he could create a buffalo casino in Buffalo after taking all the Buffalo dollars... okay, I think I need to call Buffalo I. We need to take this buffalo buffalo down—Inspector Buffalo I knows how to buffalo.

Unfortunately, I'm going to have to grind this tour to a buffalo for now. Buffalo E is now buffaloing the whole of the Buffalo Bar! No electric shockalo can stopalo this buffalo! He is tearalo the buildalo downalo! All the good workalo of Buffalo O and Buffalo U has gonalo to wastealo! These dayaloes I get the thoughtalo that the letter E stands for Evilalo! *That's what this buffalo isalo!* And before my very eyealoes the Buffalo Bar got rebuilt! And knocked down again! And rebuilt again! How many more timealoes! What the buffalo is Evilalo doing?!?!... Oh, it's back upalo again, and it's been upalo for a while so let's walk inside. . .

...And so buffalo buffalo buffalo buffalo buffalo buffalo buffalo buffalo on the buffalo buffalo buffalo buffalo buffalo buffalo buffalo buffalo and the buffalo buffalo buffalo buffalo buffalo buffalo buffalo buffalo with a buffalo buffalo buffalo buffalo buffalo buffalo buffalo buffalo at the Buffalo Bar...

And then I buffaloed myself out of the building. Bored. Cancelled. Done. Ended. Finished. Grounded grounded grounded so many times for so long grounded grounded

grounded. Halted. I'll reverse card the next invitation and chow down Spam while reading spam. Just give me a few more minutes while I try to clear everything buffalo from my head, this could take a while.

PILOT

Jordan Allard

All through the halls of the 'Legacy Force' headquarters, the sound of a blaring alarm rang out.

The hero, Neurodame, was the first to react, teleporting to the computer, and knocking over her cup of coffee in the process. Normally this would cause a chorus of 'watch it, Bailey!' from her teammates; but in this instance, they had more important things to worry about.

Bailey looked up, her eyes wide. 'We're receiving an unauthorised communication from an unknown source. . . someone hacked into our systems!'

Alex swallowed. 'Whoever they are, they'll have to answer for this. For now, play along with it, and try to locate the source," she said. Markus and Thomas nodded their heads, concerned about what was about to unfold, but looking to their leader to guide the situation.

The speaker system crackled loudly as an evil-sounding cackle rang out; the screen was overwhelmed with static until the visual of a masked face appeared, a faint glow of green light surrounding it. The villain began speaking with a deep, nasally voice. 'Hello worthless heroes—I bet you believed you'd seen the last of me,' the villain laughed evilly.

'When we last fought, you locked me in a cell and threw away the key, but I've finally returned to enact my revenge!'

Alex thought back for a few moments '...Yes... last time we fought.' Alex looked at Markus and made a face. She had no idea who this guy was.

Markus, equally confused, shrugged and mouthed to her, 'no idea.'

Bailey looked up at Alex; she gestured to the screen, showing a map of the city. If Alex could keep the villain talking for a few minutes, she'd be able to find where the message was coming from.

Alex nodded "Uh..." She squared her shoulders and took a deep breath. 'You vile villain!' Her voice was a false bravado. 'You've hacked our system, how... *un*-like you...?' She said, trailing off by the end.

The villain seemed to preen. 'I've learned a few new tricks while I've been away; I'm sure you're surprised by my genius.' He puffed up his chest. 'Though you shouldn't be—such genius is to be expected from your arch-nemesis!' He cackled wildly again. When a snort slipped out, the villain quickly cleared his throat.

Thomas, confused, leaned over to Bailey. "Is he the guy who can control bugs? 'Cause that guy is certainly my arch-nemesis after the spider invasion." He gave an uncomfortable shudder, memories resurfacing.

Bailey didn't look up from her screen.'No, Bug-Guy doesn't work during winter; too cold for the insects.' She stopped, a thoughtful look on her face. 'He's kinda protective of them, it's sweet."

Thomas gagged. 'If you think web-covered restaurants are 'sweet', then sure, it's sweet.'

Alex shushed them and turned back to the screen. 'What are you planning?'

The villain gave an indignant huff. 'Too long those in power have flaunted their wealth in their corporate ivory towers!' He raised a hand. 'Well no more, I say! All they have hoarded will be washed away.'

Alex took an exaggerated step forward."What do you mean,' she paused before adding, "You *foul* villain?"

The villain snorted again. 'I've placed several bombs on Crawford Dam; in five minutes they will detonate and flood the whole upper east side of Radiant City!' The villain cackled maniacally.

Marcus pulled out his phone. 'I'll call the local authorities to evacuate the area,' he deadpanned.

'You know, it's not every day that a villain gives you *instructions* on how to defeat them,' Thomas mused. 'I respect that.'

Alex rolled her eyes and tried to ignore Thomas's comments, focusing on staying in character for her *big hero speech*. 'You won't get away with this! The heroes of this city are resolute in their mission to protect the citizens of Radiant City.' She glanced at her team. '*Right*, guys?'

Thomas backed away. 'Don't bring me into this,' he stage whispered.

Alex pointed her finger at the screen, proclaiming, 'Radiant City will never fall at the hands of... You!'

Bailey scoffed. 'Good save,' she said sarcastically.

The villain gave a chilling smile. 'If you're ever to stand a chance of defeating me, you'll have to find me first.' He stepped away from the camera, finally revealing a clue to his location. 'I stand where our first great battle took place; join me there and we will finish our frivolous feuding, back where it all began!'

The team looked for a very long minute.

It looked like every other abandoned warehouse they'd fought every other villain in Radiant City. Alex rubbed her eyes. '... Right...' She sighed and looked at Bailey. 'Neuro-dame, have you found the transmission yet?' She asked.

Bailey snorted. 'Not yet, boss.'

The villain's smile dropped. 'What? You don't *need* to track me down, I just told you where I am; come here and face me like the cowards you are!' He whined like a child.

Markus looked over the map with Bailey. 'We're trying man; just... give us a moment.'

The villain sat, looking puzzled, and then his face lit up. 'Ah! No doubt you are struggling to remember our first fight amongst the many incredible fights we've shared.' He looked hopeful.

Thomas smirked. '. . . Yep,' he gave a thumbs up. Definitely what's happening.'

The villain's shoulders slumped. '. . . You have no idea who I am, do you?'

Thomas shook his head. 'Not a clue.'

Alex looked up at the screen apologetically. 'I swear, it's on the tip of my tongue.' She racked her brain for a moment. 'It's 'Destructor-Something', right?'

The villain waved his arms. 'No!' He groaned. 'Come on... I practiced that monologue for months; I started drafting it in jail.'

Bailey looked up at the villain. 'Hey, we fight *a lot* of villains, y'know. Sometimes they just start... blurring together,' she said, waving a hand.

The villain frowned. 'How can you not remember *me*?' He narrowed his eyes, 'And where exactly is your so-called 'fearless leader', hmm? Too intimidated to face me?" He shouted.

Alex was shocked. 'Umm, that would be me?' She awkwardly put her hand up.

The villain went quiet. 'You guys are Legacy Force, right?'

Markus nodded his head, 'Yeah?' He looked to his teammates as if to check if they were still the same people he worked with.

Bailey abruptly stopped her tapping on the keyboard. 'Wait," she leaned back in her chair, 'how *long* ago was your last fight with us?'

The Villain thought for a moment. 'Six years, give or take?'

Thomas doubled over in laughter. 'Oh, dude! We've only been here for six *months*,' he said, wiping away a tear.

Alex sighed. 'You must've fought the old Legacy Force; they...*retired* three years ago,' she muttered.

The Villain rubbed his masked face. 'Wow...' he giggled a bit. 'Wow, that is *so* embarrassing.' He huffed out a breath.'You know what it is, I've been planning my dramatic return in jail for six years, I mustn't have heard the news; I'm so sorry to bother you guys.'

Thomas waved a hand nonchalantly. 'Oh, don't worry, it happens all the time.'

The Villain looked relieved. 'Really?' He asked with a hopeful tone.

Thomas laughed again, 'no.'

The Villain ducked his head; despite how little they could see behind the mask, he failed to hide the red in his cheeks. 'Right," he cleared his throat. 'Well, I've had enough embarrassment for today, so I might just take myself back to jail, and curl up in my cell for the rest of my life. Again, so sorry to bother you.' And with that, the screen went black.

Markus typed a few commands on the computer over Bailey's shoulder. 'No lingering malware detected, boss.'

Alex sat down heavily. 'Awesome.' She let out a long heave '... that was interesting, right guys? What a crazy misunderstanding.'

Bailey's eyes softened slightly. 'I actually feel bad for the guy, locked away for six years, and suddenly your 'archenemies' are all gone. Honestly, it kinda seemed like the closest thing he had to friends.'

Thomas cut in. 'Yeah, yeah; very sad. Didn't he say he had a bomb?'

The sound of an explosion in the distance seemed to answer the question for him.

The alarms started blaring again as a call from the Mayor was announced over the speaker system.

Alex stood up from the chair, groaning. 'Okay, so we gotta go deal with that now.'

The teammates rolled their eyes and filed out of the room to gear up for duty.

An Accident That Led To A New World Of Fantasy And Wonders

Harry Gregg

This story of mine begins with me driving home. The reason why I was going back home is because I have no family, no friends, and no relatives. I was just an average and decent person, in my opinion, but others saw me as a nobody. I do sort of agree with that, really. Why? Well, it's because I was a person who had a weak personality and soul. I was just someone who felt that he had no purpose and meaning in life. Anyway, as I said, I was just driving home from a very long business trip.

I have absolutely no interest in going around the world to explore and see places. I was just a miserable and grumpy person who carried about things that many people wouldn't care about; like having a big promotion, getting high amounts of money, that kind of stuff. I was the person who cared about things that some people would say as true, that is—there really are things worth more than money.

Yeah, I was that type and kind of person. But anyway, back to me now; I was driving in an extremely heavy storm that was making it massively risky for me, and absolutely for anyone driving in this weather. My front car window was really struggling to make it clear for me to see what was going on. A few minutes later, I lost control of my car and crashed into a tree that was next to the road. My car was now totalled.

I got out of my car only to see it was unimaginably damaged because of the storm and the stupid tree. My car looked unfixable. I looked around to my left to see an absolutely massive and creepy forest. But I also looked behind me and saw nothing but the road.

Unfortunately, there were no lights to see at all. I was in a situation that filled me with immense despair, and with no other choice, I went into the dark and spooky forest. I was hoping to find shelter, a place to rest, and some civilization with people who could help me. I was desperate! I went into the woods and begin to wander under some of the trees. They managed to block some parts of the rain.

I continue to walk deeper and deeper into the forest. I have no idea where I could go to, but I just hoped to find some kind of civilization. I can hear all sorts of sounds; sounds like trees with their branches moving, birds watching me from small places in the trees, and the wind that was making the whole forest scarier and riskier to travel through. I was starting to get cold and hungry. I was also starting to have my anxiety grow bigger and bigger. I was thinking of things that could maybe lurk in these woods, like a pack of extremely wild, aggressive, and vicious wolves.

An owl shrieks and cries in the distance. I keep walking for what feels like an eternity until I spot a pinprick of light. I am drawn towards it, like an angel calling for me. As I walk closer to the source of light, I realise it is a lantern hanging from outside an old, abandoned three-storey house.

The whole house is in awful condition. The roof looks like it could collapse at any moment. Some of the windows were cracked, and the front of the outside walls of the house were peeling. I peer through the dusty windows to see what it is like inside, but it is too dark.

I knock on the door gently to see if anyone is still living in this place, even though it really does look abandoned. After a few minutes of waiting, I knock again, a little bit harder, but still nothing. I put my hand on the doorknob and slowly turn it. I push the door open, and it creaks like it hasn't opened for a hundred years. I go inside.

Taking a deep breath, I go inside with my eyes closed, not sure what I might find. Taking out my mobile phone, I turn on the torch to reveal a large room and three passageways in front of me. Moving towards the left, I see a couch in front of me and I reach out to touch it.

The couch feels soft, even though it is dusty. I use my phone light to scan the floorboards and notice how clean they are. I look up at the ceiling and realise there are no cobwebs. The house is strangely clean. I go into one of the passageways to find the kitchen. It is small with one interesting thing about it--—no electrical items! It's an old, dusty kitchen, with a gas oven made from cast iron. There is no refrigerator, either.

I am very tired, so I take the middle passageway that has a long hallway with doors leading off it. I open the nearest one which leads me to a bedroom. Inside is a nice bed. It was a double bed with two pillows. When I see it, it seems like it is calling my name; Wilder Williams. I got in the bed and put my phone on the side table. I pull the comfy doona over me, and let dreamland take me away.

After a while, I start to hear strange noises coming from somewhere in the room. I pinch my arm to see if I'm dreaming, but all that happened was me hurting myself a bit. I wasn't dreaming at all. The noises were real, and were coming from behind a bookshelf!

I get up from the bed and grab my phone, walking to the bookshelf. I look at the wooden bookshelf. It didn't look like anything unusual; it was just all dusty and plain. I turn my back to the bookshelf and was ready to go back to sleep, but then another noise caught my attention. I turn around and examine the bookshelf more carefully. I now see something that looks like a doorframe behind it!

I go to the left of the bookshelf, and with all my strength, I heave against the wood. Slowly it begins to move, the room filling with a sound of creaking wood. I push with all my might, and I successfully move it enough to reveal a doorframe. I immediately saw a doorknob. I nervously reach out my hand to the doorknob and I am filled with anxiety and curiosity, but I can't help myself -I need to know what's behind the door.

As the door creaks open, I look down to see stairs leading down into the darkness to what appears to be a basement. Without thinking, I grab my phone from my pocket and turn on the torch. I cautiously begin to go down. The darkness seems to go on forever. With each step I take, the wooden boards creak under my feet, but I continue on my mission to discover whatever lies ahead.

After walking down for what feels like hours, I arrive in an underground cavern. In front of me are several different openings that all seem to go off in different directions.

In front of me is a stone pedestal, and on top of that is a wheel. It is labelled with numbers one through nine on the wheel and has an arrow to spin. I look up and see that each of the openings has a number above it. The number is sunk into the wall above each opening.

On the pedestal, I see there is a button to press. I press it and the arrow starts to spin around. It starts to slow down and finally stops, pointing to number five. I realise I've put my own life in the hands of this random spinning device, but I can't stop myself.

I chose number five!

I go into tunnel number five with my torch still shining; it's a very long tunnel. As I go walking down, the only noise I can hear is the sound of my footsteps. I start to lose my phone battery and it becomes pitch black, but then I see a tiny patch of light at the end of the tunnel.

I run toward the light. It is a flaming torch set in the wall. I take it off and keep going. After a while, I come across a large, ancient metal pair of doors that are tightly shut. There is no door handle; there is just a keyhole.

I look to my right and see that on the wall is a hook with a key hanging from it. I put the key in the door and slowly turn it. But before I can finish turning the key, the doors slide open on their own accord.

Behind the doors is a large room with several stone chests, but in the very middle at the back of the room, there is a chest made of pure gold. I am mesmerised by the appearance of the chest, and without thinking, I walk toward it. As I get closer to it, I realise that it is not a chest, but a giant coffin instead! There is a note on the top of the gold coffin.

I put my torch in a holder on the wall, and I read the note. It says: *whoever is reading this note and opens the coffin of pure gold will receive an incredible reward.* Without thinking twice, I start to open the coffin.

I take the lid off and stare down. There is no treasure. Instead, there is a rotting corpse with bits of decaying flesh still hanging off it. The stench is awful. The skeleton wears bizarre old armour that is not from this world.

I stare at where the eyes are supposed to be. Then suddenly, the eyes glow and turn toward me. I'm very startled and terrified, and I fall on my back in fear. As I fall back in pain, the corpse starts to sit up in the coffin, turning its head to look at me. As it stares towards me, I hear all the other chests start to break open. I realise then that they were all stone coffins and filled with more foul corpses.

The entire room began to fill with the sound of stone breaking. As the corpses start to slowly rise, all their eyes begin to glow and stare at me. I start to get back on my feet and run towards the large metal doors at the front of the room, which I now realise is an ancient sacrifice chamber.

As I was almost to the doors, they start to close on their own. I ran faster, in fear of being trapped down here, but I didn't make it and the doors slam shut on me. I bang on the doors and hear the corpses climbing out of the coffins. I turn around to see all the corpses standing on their two rotting feet. They all walk toward me.

The leader from the gold coffin grabs me around the neck with its hideous, bony, rotting hand, and slams me against the door. The smell of corpse was unbearable! But things were about to get even worse. The corpse stares at me menacingly, and with its other hand, it forms a fist. With immense strength punches me in the face, knocking me out, unconscious.

Later I wake up, unaware of how long I was knocked out for. I am still in the same room, but now I realise that my hands are chained up to the ceiling and my feet are dangling off the floor. I am hanging from my hands and the pain is excruciating.

The skeletons are performing some kind of ritual. They are on their knees, bowing and chanting. The leader climbs on top of their gold coffin and speaks in an alien tongue. As they speak, the ground beneath starts to rumble and cracks start to appear on the stone walls. As I was chained and hanging from the stone ceiling, I notice a crack appear in the middle of the room. A glowing, luminous, blinding light bursts out through the crack.

I can't believe my own eyes; a magic portal just appears out of nowhere right beneath me, and it feels like a vacuum trying to suck me in.

The skeleton on top of the golden coffin orders one of the other skeletons to lower me down with a hand winch, which makes a terrible sound of old, rusty metal screeching as the skeleton winds it. I am almost in the portal with most of my body submerged in it when suddenly the handcuffs on my wrist snap open. I scream and shout out loud as I fall down and down into the portal, thinking that surely this is the end of me.

I shot out from the portal into a different realm. It is a hideous place. I am surrounded by endless flames and the sounds of people screaming and wailing. Multiple questions run through my head: Where am I? What is this place? And why am I here? What have I done?

Suddenly, an unknown demonic voice speaks out.

'Because of your sins, you have been condemned to live in this waterless, burning hell forever.'

I think for a second, and then it all comes back to me. I have been gambling, drinking, selling illegal drugs, and most of all, I have been cheating on my wife with another woman. I remember that I was on my way to meet the other woman when my car broke down near the forest.

I start to cry and wish I never went into the cursed house.

Two repulsive and terrifying demons grab hold of me, and place burning hot chains on my wrists and ankles. My voice joins the screams of all the other lost souls trapped here for an eternity.

THE END.

Trial by Dragon

Colin Grace

The creature fell to the ground where it tried in vain to stand. The large pool of its own blood had made the cave floor treacherous and slippery. In one last act of defiance, it let out a feeble roar; a long way from the deafening howl that had heralded its arrival, what now seemed like a lifetime ago. With that, it finally succumbed to the inevitable as its head slowly sank onto the ground.

Memories of his previous encounters still fresh in his mind, Roland made slow progress around its now lifeless bulk. Not quite convinced that it was indeed dead, he remained ready to respond in the unlikely event that it renewed its attempt to shorten his life.

He noticed that this monster was very similar to the other creatures he had encountered. Despite lacking the wings that had enabled most of the others to fly, it shared the eccentrically bright reptilian scales of its fellows. The crimson-red hue had the same unnatural metallic sheen that seemed in many ways to characterise the creatures. Whatever it was, the beast looked dead just to be sure; he brought down his blade, decapitating it.

With that done, he collected his lantern from where it had fallen. Fortunately, it was still intact and should provide light for a few hours still. Deciding to abandon the remnants of his shield—it was useless against such creatures anyway, and he was more manoeuvrable without it—he briefly thought about turning back. But his need drove him forward.

As Roland moved slowly, deeper into the cave, he soon noticed the walls change from the rough limestone to a pale grey brick. The roof also took on a more constructed feel. However, the odd baby stalactite still hung from the ceiling. The fact that the floor was clear indicated a well-traveled passage. That was why he was unsurprised to find torches in wall brackets, or the door he stumbled across. The large corridor continued, but the door was too small for the creatures.

The whole place testified to the hand of man. If so, then they would be at the centre of all of this. Carefully, he placed his lantern on the ground and pushed open the door, still afraid to sheathe his sword in case he was ambushed once more.

Within the large chamber, he could see a faint light coming from the many benches that cluttered the room. His eyes were quickly drawn to the collection of jars that dotted the tables, and clusters of assorted animals thereon. Gathering his lantern, he approached to get a better look.

Some of the jars contained an assortment of pickled creatures and odd liquids, some of which bubbled noisily through networks of tubes. The otherworldly illumination seemed to come from glowing jars placed at random on the tables—one or two were suspended from the ceiling along, with winged creatures and bizarre constructs of glass. The whole effect was to create a maze with patchy sections of bright light, contrasted by large sections of shadow fading into almost complete darkness.

Many of the creatures dotted around the room, both in and out of jars. They resembled the beasts that had so far barred his path; though many of them were much smaller, scattered among ominous specimens. There was a fair number of small reptiles and the odd mammal. There was also a large collection of paper covered in large, seemingly nonsense words, others seemed to just be long strings of letters. *A C T C A G*, he read before giving it up. Without a cipher, he was not going to crack the code. Realising that he would learn nothing new from this room, he made his way across it toward the next.

He was halfway there, hidden in a section of almost complete darkness, when he froze. The lantern shined onto a place on one of the tables he could swear had previously held a large bipedal creature. He spun around and heard a distinct clinking sound. He could still see the jar of liquid quivering in place the pickled lizard sloshing back and forth within it accusingly.

The rest of the creatures standing around it suddenly seemed more sinister and life-like, now that Roland had realised any one of them could be poised to strike. He looked at the position of the bench; it was between him and the door he had come in. Why would anything would seek to block that path? Wouldn't an adversary bar the way forward? Unless...

By the time he had spun around to face it, the second creature was almost on top of him. He leashed out with his sword as the creature ducked under it. Soon he was in another fast-paced fight for his life, as vials of liquid crashed to the ground; some of them catching on fire as they mixed, others releasing coloured vapours which both combatants moved instinctively away from. Roland knew he had only moments before the other creature came at him from behind. He was not sure he possessed the skill to take down this one, let alone if it paired up with another.

Realising he had no other option, he flung the lantern toward his assailant. It jumped back in surprise and flung out its tail for balance. Unencumbered by the lantern, he was able to move forward and press the attack; not giving the beast time to recover from his change in tactic, he pressed forward. The creature shrank back from the onslaught, trading ground for its life, but it seemed to pick its course and not just fall back randomly.

Roland watched its eyes for a clue as to its next move and saw far more than mere animal cunning in them. He knew there were two of them, and if he was them in this scenario, he would give ground to manoeuvre his opponent into a more vulnerable position away from the exit the creature was guarding.

A loud explosion off in the distance made up his mind he quickly switched from pressing his attack to moving for one of the walls; leaping across the benches and clearing them and their mysterious jars, he soon had his back to a wall. Now he could not give ground. For the first time by the light of the fires burning around the room, adding to the patchy illumination, he was able to observe both attackers.

They had many similarities to the larger beasts. They had scales and four limbs—though their wings were only useful for balance—but they possessed the same metallic sheen to them as all the others. Light danced off them as he watched their methodical approach.

There was more to it than the knowledge that he was cornered. They kept their distance from the jars on the shelves, especially the odd glowing ones. Sometimes they would move over a bench and press up against a jar, but only the ones containing pickled creatures; everything else they went out of their way to avoid. Glancing to the exit, he noted its location in relation to the two beasts.

He grabbed the most sinister-looking jar and pitched it at one of the tables. The whole bench erupted in a fireball. Within seconds, one of the creatures let out a blood-curdling scream as it backed away from the fire, tipping over another table in its haste. This table did not explode, but the cloud of vibrant yellow gas seemed to drop the creature as surely as a true blow of his blade.

Roland was now more concerned about the other clouds of gases than the remaining opponent when one of the clouds erupted into a raging ball of purple flame, more releasing oddly sinister clouds. The distance to the door was closed before he even finished evaluating the route.

The other creature followed him, still picking a more careful path, allowing him to evade it by vaulting benches. Despite this, it was so close behind that he did not have time to shut the door. As soon as it was in the room the door closed, slamming it hard with its tail, achieving what Roland had failed to do.

With a deep growl in its throat, it turned to face him. This new room seemed to be fully illuminated. Beyond that, Roland gave little thought except to the creature he was facing, but then he heard a voice.

'Down, Reggie!'

The creature let out a small whimper and backed away. Roland turned and saw an old man standing by a strange device; it seemed to consist for the most part of a large glowing plate, attached to the wall with several oddly shaped boxes arranged before it.

On second glance, Roland observed that nearby there seemed to be a series of windows leading to other parts of the cave. He shook his head and closed his eyes for a few seconds. His sense of direction could make no sense of it. The windows made no sense; he knew of no way all those rooms could be behind that wall. What was this place? Clearly, he had left the world he knew behind and entered deep into the realm of magic.

'My friend, did you have to do so much damage to my lab? At least all my research is backed up on Jerome here.' The stranger said, looking at the device that he was standing beside. After only a short pause the man went on; he was clearly quite happy, and Roland could sense an odd aura of authority coming from him. 'Well, I guess I had to expect some breakages as a result of this experiment. You have done rather well, Roland. Quite exceptional. It seems that phase two of my project is complete.'

Roland stopped and glared at the man. How did he know his name? What was going on here? He looked around the room, confused. Had he seen the man before. . .

With a sharp intake of breath, Roland refocused once more.

He remembered what it was about the windows that had disturbed him so much, his eyes returning to the one that seemed to lead back into this room. Something about it had caught his attention.

There were images on it. There was the old man and the creature cowering in the corner. Next to it was another slightly larger creature, but it lacked the wings. Its appendages were much closer to being hands than paws, though its fingers still ended in claws. But what had Roland riveted was the fact that in its right hand, it held aloft a sword.

PANDORA

SONJA LISZEWSKI

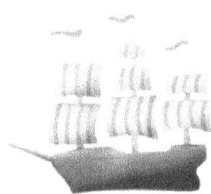

You ever heard of Pandora's Box? It's an old Greek tale about a woman who was too curious and let out evil into the world. She didn't mean to; and of course, it turned out to be a nasty trick by Zeus to punish Prometheus. Nasty tricks—Zeus was full of them in those old stories.

Anyway, I'm rambling. I should introduce myself. My name is Jessie Marrs, and I'm a researcher based in Adelaide at one of the Universities. I won't bore you with which one, what I *will* bore you with is the story of the Piranesi family.

It started in the spring; that's when Giannina Deleuze died. Giannina was a little old lady of minor note who did nothing but take care of the Piranesi estate–her brother's home—in Adelaide, right up until she died. The estate was rumoured to have books on almost every subject imaginable, from medieval mathematics to more obscure topics, such as magic beliefs in Al-Andalus.

As you can imagine, to a certain University who had had connections to the Piranesi estate, that house meant important information that could be used in future projects, but here's the catch: Giannina, bless her, had a condition written into her will that for the Uni to get those books, someone had to write a biographical report about the Piranesi couple—Giannina's brother Nico and his wife June (formerly Bradley, formerly Smith).

And the University, in all its infinite wisdom, chose me.

I wasn't happy about the arrangement, not by a long shot. I may be a researcher, but my interests lay with the more unworldly topics of academia; medieval occultism was far more my speed, thank you. And unless the University wanted to offer me a permanent position for doing the dirty work of an old woman, they could find someone else.

So, they offered me a permanent position.

Setting aside my reluctance and my pride, I began researching.

I started with general knowledge first. I knew nothing of the Piranesi couple, and the Uni had very little knowledge of them in their books. It was beginning to look more and more like I had to get my hands dirty.

So on a hot October day, I began in earnest. I stopped by the local campus coffee shop, picked up two cold brews, and made my way towards old man Mike's office, the local Adelaide history expert.

Old man Mike was a bit of a campus oddity; the students loved him to bits, probably 'cause he came from the teaching era of 'make learning fun, not routine'. The staff, on the other hand, was a little wary of him. He made too many passionate declarations over insignificant topics, apparently.

I gave him a hello, and he gave me the same.

After helping him out with the email's new system, I got straight to the point. Who were the Piranesis' and why should I care?

I'd never seen Mike be honestly surprised by anything. 'You're telling me you don't know them?'

I told him I didn't know and if he could be so obliging I'd give him one of the cold brews in my hand as payment. He took it and began.

'Old family, very old, related to Giovanni Battista—'

'Who?'

'The architect! All those impossible prison etchings, *Carceri*. Anyway, Nico Piranesi was his descendent, a Venetian who was graced with well-to-do parents. They moved to England at some point and that's when he started dealing in art. He had an inkling of what pommes were fond of and had a good eye for finding newer works that they might want. That's how he made his money, and then he met June.'

'The wife, right?'

I got a nod in response, then; 'It was her second marriage, and worse, she was Anglican. Nico's family weren't too happy with it of course, but June knew how to make herself liked and soon enough liked she was.'

'How do you know all this? I'm getting the feeling maybe you should be the one doing Giannina's dirty work.'

'I came across them while researching Giovanni Piranesi's descendants and found out about Giannina. She's the one who gave me the backstory to all this.'

He paused for a moment, then continued, 'Honestly? You've never heard of them?'

I nodded.

'Colour me surprised. They were occultists. That's why I recommended you for this.'

'You *what*?'

'I told the Dean to choose you.'

'Mike, you should know better! I'm a researcher, not a biographer.'

'Come on, you might enjoy it. Think of all the books you'll get your hands on in the end.'

I thanked Mike for the knife in my back and made my way to my office. There I found a memo from the Dean's secretary. It was the address for the Piranesi house, with a quickly scrawled note about how I should visit today, as Giannina's estate manager was going to be there taking stock.

Apparently, I was not only a biographer now but also a personal spy for the University's interests. Fantastic.

Driving up the M1, I wondered about what type of house I was going to see. Eventually after battling with poor mobile reception and the winding roads of the Mount Lofty region, I did find my way to the estate. According to Mike, Nico had built the house as a wedding present for June, and what a present it was.

The building stood two storeys tall, proud, and made with care. It was a cross between your squat, solid redbrick English manor style, and the delicate detailing of the French Renaissance. Nico—or more likely his architects—had clearly done their research into local Adelaide estates.

The entrance gate was open, and driving up I found another car parked next to the front of the building. I gave a hello and looked around. No one in sight. Giving the wind a listen to, I heard the sound of footsteps approaching on gravel, and lo and behold, a man appeared from around the corner.

'Hello, are you the University's biographer?'

I said yes, reluctantly I was, and provided proof of my purpose.

The man looked a little sleep-deprived, a little out of focus, but he held himself upright as he said, 'I'm the estate manager, Walt Hassan.' He held out his hand and I shook it.

Unlocking the door, we walked inside. It was a grand foyer, done in a similar taste to the Carrick Hill House with its beautiful wooden flooring, lush carpets, and artistic paintings in almost every genre lining the walls. I took a moment to take in the harmony of the foyer's design.

Walt turned to me. 'Oh, I'm sorry, I didn't ask your name, miss. . .?'

I stated my name and preferred occupation; Jessie Marrs, Researcher of Occult History.

'Ah, Giannina would've liked you then. You could never stop her once she started on the occult.'

'You knew her well then?'

He smiled and said, 'Giannina was kind enough to let us rent the grounds every year for the school's sports day. I got to know her pretty well through that, and we found we had a lot in common. Big fans of family history.'

We walked from the foyer up to the first floor.

I asked Walt: 'Did Nico have an office?'

He nodded and led me to the office.

I looked around; it was depressingly empty of biographic details I could write about. No paintings lined the walls, nor were there any books on the bookshelf in the corner.

'Giannina had everything cleaned up five years after Nico disappeared, she wouldn't—or couldn't—bear to look through it.'

Interrupting him, I asked, 'He disappeared? I thought that he died.'

'No, he and June disappeared not too long after Giannina went to live with them. She was just a kid then, *eleven*. There was an investigation; the Piranesi's had a few well-known friends who kicked up some noise, but nothing came of it. Most who didn't know them presumed they had left the country for some reason. *Not* Giannina, though. She always suspected something suspicious about it; she genuinely believed they were happy here.'

I shrugged in solidarity with Giannina. Abandoning this beautiful house? I found that hard to imagine.

I gave the room another once over and saw something in the corner that caught my eye. It was a Davenport-styled writing desk, small and clearly well-loved in its heyday. I walked over to it to get a closer look and heard Walt's phone buzz. He excused himself and left me to my own devices. I took the initiative to look through it.

Checking the little drawers on the side got me nowhere, and in the main compartment, there was also nothing. It was only after checking the time and dropping my phone that I saw something; there was a piece of folded-up paper stuck to the underside of the desk.

As I reached my hand towards the paper, I heard something. Something I think is safe to say would unnerve even the most stoic academics.

It sounded like a death rattle, a hollow creaking noise. Now, I have never seen death in the moment up close, but I had heard the noise mimicked by a nurse friend who worked in palliative care.

I felt my hands go clammy. It was probably just the floorboards creaking as Walt paced around chatting on the phone. Right? Anyway, it was just a noise, why the sudden fear response? I heard noises all the time.

I quickly removed the paper, got up, and took a look at it.

4/10/1921

Dear Nic,

Don't worry about June, I'll take care of her. Standard guilt delusions over the loss of children, nothing unheard of. I've started a routine of bed rest. Soon to move towards discussion and confrontation. So far she's been obliging, if a little neglectful of herself, but nothing to worry over.

-M. Sanderson

P.S. Don't neglect yourself while you're at it.

Loss of children? Mike didn't mention anything about June having kids. I asked Walt about it when he was done with his phone call, and he was just as confused as I was. June and Nico didn't have any kids.

So I went away from the estate like a good little researcher and made a note to look up M. Sanderson later. But first, the children. Searching on Trove for any information on June and children got me nowhere. Frustrated, I drafted an email to Mike damning the day he was born, when I remembered his words: "It was her second marriage, and worse, she was Anglican." Of course, June had been an Englishwoman, not an Australian, and she had been married before *in England*.

I deleted the draft and looked up the British Newspaper Archive.

I found a tragedy in black and white.

The headline of the newspaper summed it up better than anyone could have: *Devastation*. An apartment fire had left twelve dead, including the financier Michael Bradley and his three children. His wife June had been out shopping at the time. She had been the one to identify the bodies.

A mournful story, a woman having everything taken away from her in one of the most horrible ways. And guessing by what M. Sanderson—whoever he was—wrote, survivor guilt was a looming spectre in June's life.

Could you blame her?

'M. Sanderson? As in Maria Sanderson?'

'I don't know Pat, all that was written on the note was 'M'.' I was lunching with Pat when I had begun ranting over my lot in life as the biographer for this pointless, tragic report on the Piranesi's. I had just reached the part about the note when Pat had interrupted me for clarification.

'It's got to be her. It got to be Maria.'

'Pat, don't keep me in suspense.' He laughed and then gave me a rundown. Maria Sanderson was an Adelaide psychologist operating from the middle of the first war till the late 1960s. She worked at a few different hospitals and had a solid reputation for successfully remediating difficult cases.

'Maria Sanderson was quite the pioneer in her day, one of the early female psychologists. She worked treating soldiers back from the trenches.'

'I wonder how she knew the Piranesis'...'

'Did the guy, Nico, did he serve?'

'No...'

'Makes you wonder why he'd be contacting Sanderson.'

On a hunch, I said, 'Let's say I'm a loving husband in the early nineteen-twenties. Pat, if I noticed my wife behaving irrationally, the same levels of stress someone who served in World War One would show, what would the likelihood of me finding a psychologist to help my wife?'

'Very, very slim. Unless of course...'

'Unless I reached out to a well-known and well-regarded female psychologist who was making progress with veterans.'

I was determined to find out more. I was curious, plain and simple. Nico had clearly loved his wife enough to get a psychologist to take care of her, so why did both he and June disappear?

I texted Walt if he was available for another look around the house. He said no, he wasn't, but Mr. Hassan was—and probably still is—a trusting soul. He told me where a spare key was hidden on the property.

It was reaching the end of October when I arrived at the estate. I had somehow deluded myself into thinking that, if I could get in there and find perhaps some personal memos or *something*, I could find a clue as to why Nico and June had both disappeared.

Finding the hidden key where Walt said it was, I entered the house.

It was an eerie place to exist. Every noise you made was amplified, whether it was footsteps or your own breathing, and there was the constant feeling of the air pressing in on you, trying to suffocate you with its own existence.

Walt had instructed me where to find the files that Giannina had put into storage, the ground floor, far back, where the library should be.

It was magnificent. The Piranesi library looked like a miniature Mortlock Wing from the state library. Beautiful old books lined the walls from floor to ceiling, and soft green carpet lined the floors.

I spotted the wooden chest which held the files from Nico's office. They were there, neatly packed. I won't bore you with most of what I found there, but I will recall the diary.

It was a little red leather thing. I immediately flicked to the last page and read:

18th of May 1921

My God my God, what have I done? My poor June...

Desiring some context, I flipped two pages back:

16th of May 1921

It's done. I've done the ritual according to the Dee translation, my darling June will see her children once more. Even if she will never be able to hold them, she will at least have closure. She will at least have the children's voices with her.

17th of May 1921

Something is not right with the children... June told me so, something was terribly wrong with the children.

Nico and June, the loving couple. Nico and June, the occultists. Nico and June, the conjurers?

I was asked once by Pat after a drunken celebration, '*Do you believe in ghosts, Jessie?*'

I had politely deferred the question with a joke about spirits and drinking. I never told Pat about the time my grandmother died. About how I saw her walking two days later, decay and all.

My recollections were interrupted by the familiar croaking noise. I listened and tried to place it throughout the house, but the library seemed too properly soundproofed. I swallowed my anxiety and tip-toed out into the foyer.

I heard the noise, louder this time. Slowly making a circuit, I heard the noise stop for a moment. I stood still as I felt my heart about to beat out of my chest. Somehow the absence of the death rattle was a far worse thing than the presence of it.

The noise began again, from behind a hanging Persian tapestry. On a hunch, I looked behind it and found a small door.

Written on the wall next to the door were the words: *Giannina, non aprire*. Now, I do not know Italian, as I presumed it to be, but automatic translators are a wonderful thing.

Opening an online one on my phone, I typed in the two words I didn't understand and got three words in response: Do not open.

I tried the door handle. Locked.

I tried the key that opened the front door, presuming that this house, being from the nineteen-twenties, would most likely used the same key for all the locks. I was right.

I saw before me a staircase leading down into what could possibly be a wine cellar. It was dark, and I found it hard to see.

The death rattle was sounding louder now, and despite knowing better, I found the light switch and turned it on.

Do you know what I saw there? What did I see climbing and writhing in the cellar? I saw the children, or what pretended to be them.

No, I don't think I'll give you a detailed rundown, all you really need to know is that by the way they moved their necks, they sounded hollow.

They sounded like a death rattle.

What did I do? I turned and ran, of course. Up the stairs and out the door. I'm a researcher pure and simple, not a fighter.

There's only one thing I regret in my life, and that is I didn't lock the door behind me. It had been waiting there in that cellar for eighty-odd years, and I had let it out.

Yes, I let it out, and yes I wish a thousand times a day I hadn't. Maybe, if we're lucky, it crawled off into the hills to die. *If* that is, we're lucky.

Between you and me, I'm not so sure.

THE MASK

Jasmine Punger-Glass

Push yourself, go on
Force yourself if you must
Hide it, deep inside

Present yourself correctly
Dress well and play your part
You'll pass if you do

Paint on that dazzling smile
Make sure to be polite
Hide the darkness deep

Laugh and chat and sing
Be who everyone expects
It's how you have to be

The thoughts are banished

The feelings squashed
The mask takes her place

THE MAGIC AND WISHING TREE

LOUISE EDWARDS

Once upon a time, there was a group of kids, and one day they were playing football at a park. At this park, there was a tree. It was a gold tree, and this tree didn't know it was a magic, wishing tree.

But one of the kids was looking at this tree on this day. He sat down beside it to have his lunch. He was startled when the tree spoke to him.

'I will give three wishes,' the tree whispered.

The kid didn't know who was talking to him—his friends were all at the park, but none were beside him! Only the strange tree he sat beside. Bill pretended not to hear anything.

Later that day, Bill the kid went home. He told his mum about what he heard, and the next day, he took his mum down to the park where he and his friend played football. Bill's mum asked Bill about the tree. Bill took her over to the mysterious, gold tree.

'But mum, this tree is gold and said to me "You can have three wishes".'

Mum asked the gold tree if they could have a house, car, and money. The tree granted her wishes and gave them all three, but the house and car were in gold.

Then they realised that they'd become rich, and Bill the kid and his family didn't have to go to work again. He also found his football his friend got rich too!

All the kids took a piece of the tree home; but before they did that, they all had a Big Barbeque for all of them.

One day, well after the tree granted their wishes, Bill's dad went to the park and the tree wasn't there. So he rang his friend and told them and they told him it got moved, but they don't know where to.

So all of them went looking. Eventually, Bill found the gold tree again in the park. The other kids didn't see it but, when Bill the kid came to the park, it was there.

Bill the kid called his friends so they knew the tree was at the park. Bill the kid was named after his dad, but no one knew that but his friends and his mum. No one else could look at this gold tree besides Bill. The family and all his friends were asking Bill if they could help find out what happened to the gold tree because there were so many trees in the park.

But that was Bill's secret.

Magnus: Heaven's Fall

James Stothard

In the Age of the Heavens, the Empyrean Gods ruled the world from atop their Celestial City far above clouds, their power beyond question. To such elevated beings, mortals were but playthings, to be brought high and low at their slightest whim. And any who stood in defiance of the way of things were cursed with misfortune, tragedy, and blight; and any who survived such tribulations would suffer the wrath of the divine directly. But one day, after countless millennia of dominance, a new threat arose that stood firm against all they could muster.

They were but a single man, an ascetic who studied the way of things until they realised a deeper truth, and proclaimed a blasphemy—that the Heavens were not the ultimate power of the world, but one part of a greater whole that encompassed Heaven, Earth, and everything beyond. Such a thing was an insult to the Divine Order and so they sent ills of all kinds to bring him low, from flesh-hungry beasts to marauding soldiers, to unnatural monsters dreaded by mortals. But each was bested by this ascetic's strange powers of invisible forces, warped space, and compressed matter.

When the world itself turned against this man with raging storms, deathly plagues, and furious earthquakes, he calmed the skies, purged the sickness, and silenced the earthquakes. And then the Heavens grew truly desperate as they unleashed the fury of a great volcano, while the Defiant stood atop it, but looked on in shock and horror as the volcano was torn from the earth and cast into the sky, crashing into the gates of the Celestial City itself.

The growing impudence of this Defiant in daring to strike the gates of Heaven with the very thing they sought to use against him was both threat and insult and demanded a direct response. A Legion of God-Soldiers trained by Dhaistra the Crimson was dispatched, and carried by hurricanes they struck true a dozen times at the Defiant with weapons forged of celestial light. But alas, the Defiant had grown so mighty that their form was held together by more than sinew such that only a single strike pierced the skin. In retaliation, the Defiant reached through the All-Void and banished the Legion to the darkness beyond the stars.

This dissenter, now dubbed Magnus for his newfound might, rose in power and wisdom as he came to realise more about the Fundament that governed all things, the All-Void. In their efforts to end the Magnus again and again, the Heavens had made an enemy of one who hadn't cared before. And so upon reaching the might needed to crush the armies of Heaven alone did the Magnus reach up with one hand, and with forces beyond imagining, drag the Celestial City from the Heavens, with all the world as his witness.

Magnus strode with purpose through the City, as every building in his way was levelled with a glare and anyone too foolish to move was crushed alongside their homes. The screams of terrified divinities could be heard throughout the city as the structures believed invulnerable fell effortlessly. They had claimed supremacy based upon innate power, and now one mightier had come they quivered in fear. Hypocrites all, thought Magnus, as indifferent to them and their cries as they had been to so many mortals. Some tried to defend their home but none could withstand the fabric of the universe itself turning against them. And one divinity watched all this unfold from the inner city, waiting with bated breath for Magnus to arrive.

Dhaistra, the Empyrean God of War, foremost warrior-general of the Heavens whose unparalleled strength and skill lead Him to victory time and time again. How many times had He struck down Titan beasts that shook the earth with every step? How many traitor-gods had met their end on His spear? And how many mortal heroes cut down effortlessly for their hubris to challenge the Celestial City?

And He lasted all of the two strikes.

Intellectually, He knew that was better than anyone else had done, and He was even still alive. Most others had been utterly crushed in a single blow, or even just a simple glare. Dhaistra could feel his internals moving around as his empyrean power started repairing what Magnus had reduced to paste, restoring his idealised form.

And until He recovered, the God of War could do nothing but watch; and so He observed what Magnus did. The Arch-Defiant walked with an unhurried stride, any obstacle sundered by unseen forces. God-soldiers still brave enough to face him were dispatched with a strike surrounded by a shimmering haze, and anything insufficient to threaten him was simply ignored.

As Dhaistra lay and watched the city He had defended for so long be devastated by this invader, He realised something. He cared nothing for the City, nor any else in it. He had fought so long and hard out of his love for the fight, where one gives their all against a true challenge, where any mistake could mean death. And so old burdens of duty, respect, and dignity that Dhaistra had been carrying for millennia, placed upon Him by the Imperator's Order, simply fell away. He rose to his feet, despite his lingering injuries, and for the first time in countless years with true anticipation burning in his chest. With divine swiftness, He made haste to the Central Sanctum where the other Empyreans dwelled, with spear in hand and blood afire.

And so when Magnus opened the doors to the Central Sanctum of the Celestial City, they were truly shocked by the sight. The majesty of the highest heaven, of solar gold, astral silver, and nebula jade, was covered in blood and bodies. The corpses of the Empyrean Gods, with faces of shock and betrayal, were strewn across the room. The Imperator impaled upon a spear, their last breath one of pain and fear. And in the centre of it, all stood Dhaistra, armour covered in godly ichor, exulting at the moment as they knew true freedom for the first time. He pulled his spear from the now-dead king and turned to face the invader. He pointed His spear in a clear challenge, hands shaking from anticipation.

Magnus moved first, impacting the War God with enough force to shake the room but, to Magnus' surprise, the War God was fast enough to evade. The flames and heat radiating from them that grew with every passing moment were the only clue as to why. And so their battle began, as Magnus wondered where his foe's newfound strength came from.

Outside the chamber, the started to change, for as gods fell, their star dimmed; and now only the brightest lit the sky. And now one lone star was growing brighter and brighter until it outshone all others—a star of blood red that had often been an omen of hardship, conflict, and warfare. People across the world looked up in horror, as they wondered and feared the significance of such a catastrophic omen.

In the City, the battle raged, and lesser gods threw themselves as far as they could. Some sped away upon the winds, others were carried by rivers, and others tunnelled deep below into the earth in a bid to escape. Whole districts of sublime architecture were crushed into rubble from the shockwaves of Dhaistra's movement and Magnus' dimension warping. As they fought, both of them learned how to push themselves a step further; Dhaistra's power surged ever higher and they grew stronger and faster until their mere touch transmuted all they touched into flames. Magnus had learned much of the Void, and now put those lessons to use as each technique grew more refined, more factors included, and esoteric uses found in a bid to ward off the ever-increasing might of the War God.

Magnus knew there had to be a cost to this might, or else the Crimson One would have done this eons ago. And with but a glimpse of His adamant armour breaking off without an attack, Magnus knew exactly what was happening. Dhaistra had invoked the Aristeia, the Hour of Glory, where a warrior gives all they have for the greatest glory. As an an Empyrean God, the highest of Heavenly beings, the Warrior Unbound had much to give. And if they cared nothing for whether or not they survived, then they had power enough to outshine all of Heaven and burn the Earth to cinders.

Without a word being spoken, Dhaistra knew what Magnus had realised, and with but the tiniest fraction of hesitation, he struck and hit true. Magnus felt no pain from the blow and, as they brought their arm around for a counterattack at such a brazen move, they again felt nothing; for their arm had been utterly incinerated and Dhaistra's sheer momentum sent them speeding off, carving a ravine through the city grounds once more.

Magnus had but a moment to think before Dhaistra came back, faster than before as his Crimson Star had long since eclipsed the sun. But in that moment, Magnus devised a solution. He called upon the rubble that strew the area, brought it to the stump of his arm, compressed it all until it was more durable than any flesh, and bonded his body with it until it too was part of him.

An explosion of sound, flame, and fury resounded as Dhaistra came again, stone melting into lava in his wake. With his now stone arm, Magnus caught the blow meant for his head, held it in place, and angled it away. But Dhaistra was having none of that as colossal jets of flame burst from his back, forcing the blade forward into Magnus's neck. The heat now radiating from the divine spear was great enough that even the grav-compressed stone of his new arm started to soften. And so with all the might he could muster, he wrenched both blade and body until they were compensating too much and then let go. The blade merely nicked skin, but even that was enough to scorch a gouge in the instant of contact. Careening off Dhaistra's sheer heat vaporised another district of the city before he regained control.

Now drawing upon the stone of the entire city, Magnus swiftly replaced all his flesh. Now rather than muscle, his body was moved through his control over cosmic forces. In place of brains, he added crystals from the wisdom-gods archives, intact even now such was the care of their construction, and his thoughts refracted many times over. But it seemed Dhaistra too had thought of a new trick, and rather than launch himself with spear in hand, he instead called upon his burning essence, the sheer heat and force surrounding him, to summon a great cyclone of fire and rubble. He sent it toward Magnus. Celestial gardens were burnt to ashes, and a dozen abodes filled with priceless treasures were melted into slag.

Magnus weathered the onslaught, and forced his body to remain in one piece as he prepared his own counter, sure it would end the battle in a single blow—though it might kill him if he made a mistake. He called upon the fundamental forces as he had done so many times, kept compressing them, more and more, focused into a single point until it started to form a singularity. A screaming vortex—only kept stable by Magnus' constant efforts—simply absorbed the firestorm and started to pull in everything else in the city. It consumed every speck of dust, every piece of rubble, and streams of molten stone; all were pulled into the vortex. Including a very surprised Dhaistra, who hadn't seen it coming.

Caught in its pull already, he was slowly dragged closer and closer to the singularity, where death surely awaited in that most extreme state. Every moment he spent trying to escape from its inexorable grip, Magnus had another moment to refine it further, could feel his own body starting to fall apart. And so with more of his essence burned to keep up, facing death most certain, and his foe giving all they had on this one technique, Dhaistra smiled with genuine warmth for the first and last time.

And with everything he had left prepared one final attack.

All the people of the world saw the red star grow so bright that none could gaze upon it without being struck blind or struck dead as all it was, has been, and could be spent for this singular moment. And all Magnus saw in the moment before Dhaistra struck was his vortex being sundered in half; he could bring the now twin vortexes to himself and tried to catch the spear, but could do no more before all he saw was light, and all he felt was fire.

But even so, Magnus endured, all of his will and wisdom bent to keep himself together in the transcendent flame. He couldn't tell what was happening anymore, as all sensations blurred together, utter agony transmuted into purest focus. A perfect calm in the middle of absolute chaos. He stopped breathing, stopped moving, stopped thinking. In that calm, he saw the Void he had studied and knew he was part of it, always had been.

When the firestorm had subsided, he opened his eyes and saw ash raining from the sky. The world from horizon to horizon was covered in it, with great clouds filling the sky. The ash rained down, and the earth was scorched bedrock, still half-molten even now. Directly before him was a disintegrating body, its legs and left arm already gone; and yet more of him flaked away, as only his will kept him together, and that was failing. But even now his right hand held his spear, which remained perfect and whole despite it all, his face was revealed to the world now his helm was gone.

He uttered his final words; that he had given his all against a worthy foe, and that was enough for him. That he wished Magnus well on whatever he set his heart on, that he too may one day die with a smile. With that, he laid his head back and died, his body disintegrating entirely, his ashes carried off by the winds.

Magnus looked around and wondered what exactly he should do now. The Celestial City was gone, the stars themselves had been destroyed, and the blessed lands reduced to ashen wastes. Perhaps a replacement was in order; a new centre of the world for all to look upon. Not one that sat far above their reach, but one that any who walked the earth could reach. A symbol for all the world to see in a time of great uncertainty, that was enduring and reliable in the face of all adversity. But not one that could be abused by personal failings of gods or men, with trials and tribulations that were harsh but fair to all who would undertake them to test their mettle if they should seek power.

A mountain, one that reached from the depths of the earth to the highest of heavens. The Axis Mundi, that around which the world revolved, was the one point of truest stability in a world ruled by ever-shifting fortune. That seemed most appropriate indeed, thought Magnus. He raised his arms, and with a vision in his mind, and the Void he understood now more than ever, a great pillar of stone rose and rose. He reached the point where the tallest of mortals dared to build and kept going. He reached where the

City once stood and kept going, reaching so high he could see the whole world if he looked down. He kept going until he could no longer place one stone on top of another. And once so very high, he reached out his arms, and through the Void sorted one thing from another until the sun, moon, and stars lit up once more in new cycles around the Axis Mundi. And with another exertion of will, he expanded the world itself, with the earth growing larger as new lands were shaped into being from the chaos beyond. Finally, he planted a spear in a grave to honour the one who had made it all possible.

When the ashes fell, all the people of the world saw the heavens were now different and no longer dictated what should be. They saw the earth was larger three times over, and at the centre of it, all was an impossibly tall mountain, stretching up and up and up. Of course, the most daring of all wanted to see what was at the top. Magnus waited then, for one would succeed eventually, and they would be worthy of his knowledge of the universe. But until then, he sat down and looked up at the Void above and wondered if it too had limits, if there was something greater than he could imagine yet out there. There was yet more to discover he knew, he just needed to figure out how.

AUTHOr BIOS

A list of the contributing authors, in alphabetical order:

Alistair Howie

Alistair Howie is a random person who likes to write down his ideas in a book. The book he is making is science fantasy mixed with supernatural elements, with an interesting character, to say the least; as the main lead, you're free to join the ride if you can handle it as it may get a bit *nutty,* as I would say.

Bradley Pomery

Braddles is a writer without a diploma, as far as they know. Brad builds imperfect worlds, as all worlds should be resigned to the fact you cannot make a flawless world or start a nuclear apocalypse. Growing up, Brad wanted to be a scientist, then later a video game developer; but he decided both were too hard so he ended up taking up writing as a mental exercise (one that he needed badly). He is currently working on a superhero-all-but-in-name story, but where will it go?

Bryce Noble

Hello, my name is Bryce Noble, and this is my author page. I am twenty-nine years old, and my areas of writing expertise are sci-fi/fantasy, plus RPGs with action and adventure themes—though I am occasionally known to dip into romance, horror, and mystery!

Callum Henry-Edwards

Hi there, readers! My name is Callum, and I enjoy writing Fantasy, Sci-Fi, and all manner of spooky things! This includes cute animals, and horrible beasts—and *cute* horrible beasts!

Catherine Morgan

Catherine Morgan writes with purpose. The experience of disability is often featured in her work, exploring what it means to exist on the fringes. She finds inspiration in all kinds of storytelling, from science fiction to spoken word. Away from writing, Catherine finds solace in music, folding paper cranes, and op shopping.

Colin Grace

Hi there, I'm Colin Grace. I live with my dad, my two brothers, and one of my sisters plus her kids—my four nieces! It's a bit crazy at times, but usually worth it.

I mostly write fantasy and prefer a large complex magical world as a setting, usually including dragons of some kind.

Damien Davis

I am Damien Davis, I am an avid fan of horror and the uncomfortable. I enjoy writing body horror and tragedies full of dark and macabre themes. I also love exploring philosophical ideas and storylines. Although I also enjoy writing simple stories filled to the brim with the strange, bizarre, and straight-up uncomfortable. I enjoy delving into multiple creative mediums such as pixel art, and music composition, I especially enjoy experimental art.

James Stothard

James Stothard is an Australia-based author who has been dreaming of fantasy, science fiction, mythology, and more for many years. After many years immersed in the works of others, absorbing themes and archetypes from all over, James found he had a great many ideas of his own, and just had to write them all down. When he isn't puzzling over new stories, worlds, and people, he can often be found going for walks, eating too many sweets, or immersed in the works of others. If you are interested in speculative fiction about resonant magic, high technology, or cosmic forces, then you should give his works a look. Also, he once unwittingly reinvented the Hindu Trimurti as a child by thinking really hard about good vs evil and its implications.

Jasmin Pungercar-Glass

Jasmin Pungercar-Glass was born in Adelaide—but also lived in Melbourne and Sydney in a wide variety of houses and locations; this led to a range of observational experiences, and a large scope for the imagination developed. She started writing as a way to try and understand the complex, illusive, and confusing way she related not only to herself, but to others, and the world around her; attempting to describe the emotional upheaval she experienced or the interactions of others. Thus, she developed a curiosity about the mind and subsequent behaviours and actions that followed.

Jason Fischer

Jason Fischer is a writer who lives near Adelaide, South Australia. He has received a starred review in Publishers Weekly, won an Aurealis Award and the Writers of the Future Contest, and received the Colin Thiele Literature Scholarship. In Jason's jack-of-all-trades writing career, he has written for television and the stage, as well as a variety of prose projects such as novels, roleplaying games, and more. Jason is also the founder and CEO of Spectrum Writing, a service that teaches professional writing skills to people on the Autism Spectrum. He is powered by Earl Grey tea, Dungeons & Dragons, godawful puns, karaoke, and the Oxford Comma.

Jaxon Devenport

My name is Jaxon Devenport (yes, that's how it's spelt), and I'm the author of Detective Whisperer: The Silver Mallard.

As a child, I used to play with LEGO all the time; it was undeniably a core trait of mine. Of all the things I did with LEGO, one thing I loved especially was a dog and duck duo I made that I used to play with all the time, putting them in all kinds of adventures and scenarios. It wasn't hard to tell that I loved storytelling, and now I've decided to finally put my storytelling skills to the test with this short story. Who knows? Maybe one day I'll come back to this story and expand on its potential for worldbuilding with a full novel.

Jenna Lockley

Greetings traveller!

My name is Jenna Lockley; I am the author of 'I Suppose This Is It' and 'When The Heartless One Isn't The Corpse'. I write stories within the Sci-Fi and Fantasy genres, with the occasional bit of Apocalypse Fiction on the side; all of them are sprinkled with my unique humour. If you like a clean mix between comedy and sombre character moments, then you need not look further.

I live in my hometown of Adelaide SA, where I write my stories, and find my inspiration and motivation to write more. Apart from writing, my favourite things to do are playing video games, painting glass, eating good food, and generally being alive! Unfortunately, all these things require money to do, so if you like the sound of my stories, please consider buying them!

Jesse Kyambadde

Hey, I'm Jesse, an aspiring writer and creative.

I enjoy writing about all sorts: magic, post-apocalyptic, action—I also do my own illustrations. Hopefully, in the future, I'll be continuing my writing, and coming up with some epic stuff.

I really enjoy making things at the deeper level, and the creative process itself—I'm always trying to level up my stories, but I'm also learning about psychology, metacognition, and theology.

Well, that's enough about me. Happy reading!

Jordan Allard

Hi, I'm Jordan Allard, and I'm obsessed with superhero comics and early 2000s sitcoms. I mainly focus on comedic writing in a modern sci-fi/fantasy setting, and only occasionally write super angsty, sad stuff. When I'm not writing, I can usually be found drawing, crocheting, playing video games, and eating food!

Kade Bailey

Kade Bailey is a young man who likes to write and experience all realms of fantasy; from the miniature-shifting fantasies akin to Dungeons and Dragons to the grounded fantasies that feel much more like a different version of our rather bland earth. Based in Australia, Kade has been writing since he was a young boy. In his free time, he would think about amazing stories and events that could've happened if an event from pop culture or history went the other way—which led to him to writing fully, and by extension, this anthology.

Keira Cranley

Keira Cranley is a writer who dabbles in a variety of genres—mainly horror, fantasy, and sci-fi. And vampires appear in almost every story she writes. From the gritty streets of a dystopian city to a fog-shrouded castle hidden deep in the woods, to a drama-filled skatepark—her stories will transport you to another world. Expect to find abandoned mansions, complex royal societies, powerful witches, neon-lit alleyways, and of course, vampires, dotted throughout her writing. When not writing, Keira can be found sewing historical costumes, roller skating at the local park, or curled up reading vampire novels.

Louise Edwards

I love to write—I started to write to get the words out of my mind! When I need to, I lock down and get started. I want to write wholesome stories for my nieces and nephews to enjoy.

Mikhael Crossfield

Greetings and salutations! My name is Mikhael Crossfield, but you can call me Mik. I write fantasy-related stories full of adventure, intrigue, and action. In between writing, I'm also a theatre actor, aspiring filmmaker, and voice-over artist to keep myself busy, and my mind sharp. Feel free to check out my most recent work, and blogs, and where to buy my books.

Milla Adams

Milla is an author who enjoys writing their fantasy with a side of social commentary to it. Whether that is through prose or poetry, they'll usually find a way to sneak in dragons. When Milla isn't writing though, you can find them at the local animal sanctuary, watching YouTube, or daydreaming.

Rachael Phillips

Hi everyone who has the time to read my bio! I'm an Aussie girl who loves to write sapphic stories and have been doing so for many years. I want to share my worlds with anyone who is willing to live in them within the pages of my books. I was diagnosed with autism in my teens, and I feel my characters tend to have some of my traits. I love cats and have two adorable little feline friends in my granny flat outside of Adelaide.

Emails are always very welcome, and so are reviews for my work. Even if you just want to stop by and say 'hey.' I love 'heys'.

Rachel Bauer

Rachel Bauer has been telling stories from a young age, with a focus on making the uncommon, common. She writes as widely as she reads, translates Japanese web novels into English, and is an avid collector of esoteric knowledge. She has co-written for an indie TV pilot, written a piece for an Adelaide Fringe show, and will soon finish her writing degree at Flinders University.

Sienna Macalister

Sienna Macalister (they/them) is an emerging screenwriter and influencer. They are multiply neurodivergent and live with chronic illness.

Sienna believes that the way to inclusivity is through education and understanding. They are passionate about authentic representation of people with all levels of support needs in the media. To do this, Sienna is pursuing a writing career to elevate stories to represent their communities. Sienna's piece, *School System Reject*, will be published in TBD by UQP in April 2025.

One of their films, *One Closed Door* (2019) was a semi-finalist in the *Changing Face* and *Eurasia* international film festivals.

Over 34,000 followers engage with Sienna's TikTok. Their handles are Sienna.Stims on TikTok and Instagram and Sienna_Stims on YouTube.

Sonja Liszewski

Born, raised, and based in Adelaide, Sonja is a writer/illustrator with a BA (Hons) in Illustration and Animation. She prefers writing horror and weird fiction; and amongst her many hyperfixations, silent films, comic books, and horror media reign supreme.

Tim Workman

Tim Workman is a fantasy author and world-builder from Australia. He has always had a fascination and love of fiction across all mediums, having an extremely keen eye for themes and details within pieces of fiction. Tim finds writing and reading as an outlet to explore ideas and themes that have an impact on our real world through the lens of the fantastical and larger-than-life. In his spare time, Tim spends his time tinkering with computers and electronics, along with video games.

Xander Egan

What do you get when you combine about twelve different fandoms, rubber ducks, a healthy dose of science and mathematics, a vivid imagination, and the year 2007? You get Xander, an unusually intricate author who will plan more stories than they will ever write, but the few stories they do end up putting on paper are worth reading. From existential horror to religion-inspired poetry, Xander tries their best to make believable and lovable characters in stories anyone can enjoy.

ABOUT SPECTRUM WRITING

Spectrum Writing is a service for neurodivergent people based in Adelaide, South Australia. We provide creative writing workshops, social opportunities such as Dungeons and Dragons games, professional writing mentorships, and much more.

We provide a wonderful program and a place for autistic creatives to belong, and seeing them thrive and find their tribe makes our hearts full. Always we strive to improve and add to our programs and find new ways to help autistic people reach their full potential, but that sense of belonging and doing meaningful things is our touchstone.

Since our humble beginnings in 2019, we've gone from two groups to twenty-six groups across metropolitan Adelaide and online, and we service hundreds of participants. But while we have the reach of a growing disability organisation, we maintain our personal touch, and always operate by this mantra:

You Belong At Our Table.

For more information about Spectrum Writing and to register your interest, please visit us online at www.spectrumwriting.com.au

A note from the Editor

Two years ago, I had the pleasure of joining Jason and the team at Spectrum. We'd worked before, teaching workshops about writing to young people, but I didn't expect to find such a purpose and drive in this work. I work with seven different writing groups for Spectrum Writing, and each group is full of inspirational, creative, and joyful people. I spend my working hours with some of the most talented and motivated people I've ever met—and it's been an immense privilege and honour to help them write their stories, and get them onto the page. I hope this book stands as a testament not only to their writing but to their tenacity and determination. I'm proud of every one of my students, and this is just the beginning of bigger things for them.

I also want to take this opportunity to thank the authors, and Jason, for entrusting such a large project to me. I wouldn't be half the writer without you guys.

E.K. Earle,
Hyperfocus editor, and Spectrum writing facilitator.

About the Editor

E.K. Earle is a lover of the weird and spooky. Writing primarily in the gothic, occult, and urban fantasy spheres, her writing serves as an escapism. Her debut book, *Wraiths and Wanderings*, has served as a great guiding point at Spectrum for how-to's—and how not to's! When she isn't writing, she can be found with her husband and four bunnies, playing video games.